# Night Swimming

Anne Eton

This paperback is also available as an ebook at most online ebook retailers.

Copyright 2013 Beginnings Press

ISBN-13: 978-1-62602-027-6

ISBN-10: 1626020276

"Hello. The temp agency sent me."

The expressionless girl standing at the door spoke in a French accent. She was mid-twenties, of average height, with long strawberry-blonde hair; a button nose complimented the surrounding freckles, giving the girl a wholesome quality. Her business jacket and skirt were stylish and tailored to her athletic build. The overall impression was of a healthy, upper-middle-class young woman who happened to be beautiful. She would have been the perfect model for a Lands' End or Brooks Brothers photo shoot—if only she would smile.

The woman who had opened the door did smile. She was perhaps twenty years older than the girl, but clearly ate and exercised carefully. She had retained her youth's beauty. A stylish knit dress hugged her curvy figure. Her bust seemed slightly too big for her body, but otherwise she looked like she could model, too. The woman brushed her long brown hair over one ear and stepped aside.

The temp girl crossed the threshold, entering the spacious house. Her host closed the door. The girl looked around. Instead of a box layout, the walls curved around like a shell's. The furniture all matched. Clearly an interior designer had had his or her way with the place—the sofa, chairs, and cabinets were elegant and perfectly proportioned in relation to each other, with a unified modern feel.

A heavy Asian woman in a T-shirt and sweatpants approached.

"YuLing, this is Laurence," the lady of the house said to her before turning back to the girl. "It is Laurence, isn't it?"

"Yes."

"Am I pronouncing your name correctly? LOW-ron-s?"

"Yes, that is right."

"YuLing is my housekeeper." She turned to YuLing: "This is the girl who will be helping me."

YuLing nodded, beaming. "You like something to drink?" she asked with a Chinese accent.

"No, thank you."

"Then I will go," the housekeeper said to her employer. She nodded to the girl, smiled again, and walked away.

The temp gazed around once more. The home

was so spotless and of such impeccable taste, it seemed ready for an episode on HGTV. However, there were no personal touches—no photographs, paperbacks, or anything to indicate that a human being actually lived in it. The girl stared out the front window. A strong surf crashed and roared between the house and white sand.

"Nice, isn't it?"

Laurence looked at the woman. "It is very nice," she said in her soft French accent.

"I really mean the ocean. The house is nice I guess, but it's a rental. I don't like it very much, actually. I chose it only because it's oceanfront. If you're in Malibu, oceanfront is the place to be. Don't you think?"

The French girl stared with steady eyes. "If one has the money."

Her hostess cocked her head. After a moment, she smiled. "Why don't we go upstairs and I'll show you everything."

They ascended spotless stone steps that hugged the curved wall. "What part of France are you from?"

"Toulouse."

"I've never been there. Is it nice?"

"Yes."

"How familiar are you with Canadian French?"

"The agency asked me this also. If I'm speaking to a French Canadian, they may sometimes have an accent that is difficult for me to understand, especially if they are provincial. But if I am reading, or writing, it is no problem. There are slang terms, but there are slang terms in Canadian English also."

"You may be speaking to a few people, but they will all be in cities. Montreal and Québec. But mostly you'll be reading documents in French."

"Then it is absolutely no problem."

They reached the second floor and walked down a hall. The older woman ushered Laurence into an office filled with received DHL boxes. A large desk covered with papers faced a floor-to-ceiling window with a spectacular view of the Pacific Ocean. A smaller shiny desk sat off to the side. It did not match any of the other furniture in the house.

"I bought your desk yesterday," the woman said. "The computer people are coming tomorrow, so you should be totally set up next time you come. Did your agency tell you the hours?"

"Monday, Wednesday, Friday, nine to noon."

"Right. So! Let's get situated."

The woman gestured to Laurence to have a seat at the smaller desk. Then she eased herself into her own chair at the big desk that overflowed with photocopied documents.

"Before we get into it, do you have any questions right off the bat?"

"How should I address you?"

"My name. Of course. I'm so sorry. Call me Peggy." She stood and offered her hand, leaning across her desk. Laurence stood also, tilted toward her, and they shook before sitting again. Peggy continued: "I should mention, since you'll see plenty of paperwork with my name on it, that Peggy is not my birth name. I was born Rebecca Roth. I changed my name to Peggy Hamilton when I moved to L.A. about, oh, fifteen years ago? I was married once after that, my married name was Peggy Goldstein. So you have to worry about remembering my married name too, ha. My name's back to Peggy Hamilton now."

"I see."

"Any other questions?"

The French girl shook her head.

"Then I'll get right to it. My father died recently."

"I'm sorry."

"Thanks." Peggy's lip trembled. "He was a wonderful man. I'll tell you more about him some time, if ever you're interested. But anyway, he was Canadian. He had extensive business holdings all over Canada and his will says everything gets split six ways. Every business, every stock, every bond, gets divided by six. He had six children, with my mom and three other wives. It gets pretty complicated." She paused.

"I was raised mostly in New York," Peggy continued. "My mother divorced him when I was little, and I was the only child. So I never really learned French. Well, I learned a little in school but I've forgotten it all now."

"A shame."

Peggy realized Laurence was making a joke. "Do you ever smile?"

The girl shrugged.

"So. I went to the funeral last week, in Ottawa, and all us kids met with the executors. His estate's a mess. I have income statements, asset valuations, contracts, letters, all kinds of crap, and boxes of it are in French and I have no idea what it all means. And that is just the stuff from French Canada, from Québec province. There's tons of other business documents from all over the country. I don't even want to talk about Alberta. You ever hear of oil sands?"

Laurence shook her head.

"Me neither, till last week. Anyway, there's boxes and boxes. The executors made six sets of photocopies of documents from my totally disorganized dad's office and mailed copies to all of us. And more boxes keep coming every day." She gestured at the cardboard containers everywhere. "Honestly, it's killing me."

A shadow crossed Peggy's face. Laurence could see a brave front disappearing for a moment, revealing an overwhelmed, frightened woman.

The girl's eyebrows knitted. "Can you hire an attorney? Or an accountant, perhaps?"

"I will. Once I've figured out what everything

is, at least vaguely. But I don't want to just hand everything off to the suits. My father would have killed me. He always told me: don't ever just leave your business to anybody, Becca. When it comes to money, trust people, but always watch them like a hawk."

"This seems... a big project."

"Yeah. And I have to figure it all out fast. Me and my brothers and sisters are meeting again in Ottawa in six weeks. I don't even know some of them. I don't know what they'll say. At the funeral there was talk of horse trading—I'll give you this, you give me that." She shook her head. "I can just see my dad somewhere now, grinning. He loved stuff like this."

"How?"

"Negotiations, business, pressure. He would have wanted me to be on top of my game, and walk away with the biggest piece of the pie."

"At the expense of your brothers and sisters?"

"Oh yeah. He actually hated some of his kids."

"Then... why divide everything equally?"

"Because he was a fair man. And maybe just a little devilish. He would have eaten this up—all his kids arguing over a table, wheeling and dealing, trying to get the better of each other."

"Oh."

"I know I make him sound like a terrible person. But he wasn't. He was the sweetest, kindest..."

Peggy stopped. She blinked, looking away at

the ocean, about to cry.

"Let's begin," Laurence said quickly. "What can I do?"

At noon, Peggy rose. "You are great. I mean it. You're awesome."

Laurence stood also. "Thank you."

"You can wear whatever you want next time. Come barefoot, if you like."

The girl nodded. She followed Peggy back downstairs. At the door, the older woman turned to her employee. "The temp agency said you were going back to France in a couple of months."

"Yes. But not before your big meeting."

"I guess if I need you after the meeting, there's always Skype, huh?" Peggy joked.

As usual, Laurence did not smile. "I am getting married."

"Congratulations. That's wonderful."

"So if I work on Skype perhaps you must hire my husband, also."

Peggy studied her carefully. "You know... I think you're funny. But I'm not sure." A thought occurred to her. "How's the setup in the office? Anything else you need, besides the computer?"

"File folders would help. And hanging files. And some filing cabinets."

Peggy departed and returned with a credit card. She handed it to the girl.

"What is this?"

"AmEx. Get on the net and go to Staples or Amazon or whatever and order it. Get it all delivered here, soon as possible. Do it under my name."

"Are you sure?"

"Yep. I'll add another hour to your timesheet."

"Today is Wednesday. So I will see you Friday. Do you want me to arrive before nine?"

"No, nine's fine. Thanks Laurence. See you Friday."

On Friday, Laurence arrived exactly on time. She wore sandals, shorts and a tight Hooters T-shirt. She looked like a waitress.

"You're kidding," Peggy said. "Do you know what Hooters is?"

"They sell owls?" The letters and logo on the shirt made the two Os into an owl's eyes.

"No, it's a restaurant where…"

"Yes, I know," the girl deadpanned. "It was a joke."

"You're something else. C'mon, a ton of boxes from Staples arrived. Thanks, by the way."

Soon, Laurence had set up the cabinets and invented a filing system.

"If on the labels we put the business name first," she said, bending over Peggy's desk to point at a paper, "and the province, and the approximate value of the company, we can use that for the hanging files. This document, for example, would be in United Timber-Manitoba-x. We can write in pencil and fill in the x later. And then we use manila sub-files inside the hanging file. Correspondence, stock reports, et cetera."

"You are amazing. Let's do it."

"We should organize all the paper first, then read it after. It will save time."

"Brilliant."

"I thought about this all of yesterday."

"I can tell. Thank you!" Peggy checked her watch. 11:55 AM. "Crap. Noon already."

"I can stay, if you want," Laurence said.

"Are you sure?"

"Yes, no problem."

"Okay. We'll knock off at five. My father always used to say that: 'knock off.'"

"It means… quit?"

"Yeah."

"Or maybe, kill?"

"Not what I meant, but, yeah, I guess that too."

A few minutes after five, the women stood by the front door.

"Thanks again."

"You're welcome. Thank you for signing my timesheet."

"Now I know you're kidding."

"If you wish, I can work nine to five, five days a week, and weekends if necessary. You have more work to do than I anticipated."

Suddenly, Peggy leaned in and kissed Laurence on both cheeks.

The French girl studied her as impassively as always. "Yes?"

"That's what French people do, don't they?"

"When saying hello or goodbye, sometimes."

"Sorry. I'm just so glad you're here. Is there somewhere you have to be right now?"

"No… do you want to work some more?"

"Hell no. Every day around this time, I have a Manhattan out by the pool. Want to join me?"

The girl looked uncertain.

Peggy pressed: "Come on! I want to learn about you. You're fascinating. And I make an incredible Manhattan, you won't believe it."

"You make margarita?"

Peggy blinked. "Yes, I do. Tell you what. Head out to the pool." Peggy pointed to the rear of the house. "I'll go take care of the drinks and I'll meet you there in a minute."

"I can't stay long…"

"Sure."

*   *   *

Laurence blinked as she stepped into the pink hues of a West Coast sunset. An Olympic-sized pool had a small adjacent hot tub next to it. The entire outdoor patio area was only slightly higher than the beach that butted up. Across the sand, ocean waves crashed.

The French girl smiled, listening to the roar. Warm wind fluttered her long strawberry-blonde hair.

"Finally, a smile." Peggy approached from the rear of the house, carrying two drinks. She wore a beautiful embroidered kimono. She seemed relaxed. Clearly, this was her favorite place and her favorite time of day.

"Thank you," Laurence said as she accepted her margarita. Condensation had appeared on the outside of the icy glass. The French girl's tongue darted out, tasting the crushed salt on the rim. She sipped. "Very nice."

"Thanks."

Peggy sat on a teak chair between the pool and hot tub. Laurence did the same.

"So I have to ask," Peggy said. "What were you smiling about just now? Since none of my jokes ever seem to work."

"I was thinking, finally, California." The French girl looked out at the ocean. "This is what I imagined California would be."

"Didn't live up to your expectations, huh?"

"No."

They talked. Laurence had finished business school in France, but could not find a job there. The economy, she explained. So, she had decided to travel. She had always wanted to visit California, and had found a long-term youth hostel for a three-month stay.

"So you've been here a month?"

Laurence nodded. "And then, my money... pouf." She made a gesture with her fingertips, showing it blowing away. "So I registered with the temp agency for part-time work."

"On a tourist visa?"

"They arranged it, somehow."

"I feel terrible. Taking up your vacation. You should be enjoying yourself..."

"It is all right. I have already seen most of the sights. And I do not have money anyway to travel far from Los Angeles."

"How did you get from your hostel to here?"

"The bus."

"Oh, no."

"It is not far. The hostel is in Malibu."

"Oh."

The conversation paused. Laurence closed her eyes. The wind ruffled her hair again. She smiled.

"You like the sun, huh?" Peggy said.

"Yes, and this is so nice."

"I love it too. I love it here." The older woman stood up. "Mind if I sunbathe?"

"What?"

Peggy's kimono dropped to the tiles underfoot. The hourglass woman stood in what was clearly a custom-made bikini. Settling back in her chair, she smiled. "I do this every day. If the sun's too high, it hurts your skin."

Laurence stared. Peggy's body was as toned as a twenty-year-old's. She looked spectacular. Her chest was even larger than it had appeared when she was wearing her clothes. No wonder the bikini was custom.

The older woman caught her guest staring. "Really something, huh?" she joked, shaking her breasts.

The French girl turned away, embarrassed.

"I almost got reduction surgery, years ago." Peggy closed her eyes.

After a pause, Laurence asked: "Why did you not?"

"My dad. He wouldn't hear of it. Don't get me wrong, it's my body and if I had really wanted to do it, I would have. But he kept saying, 'Why don't you like yourself? You're perfect.'"

"I see."

"And, you know, now? I think he was right. These things never gave me back pain, or anything. They're part of me. I like them." She smiled down at her cleavage, adjusting the fabric's hem with her finger.

"I should go." Laurence rose. "Thank you for the drink."

"Welcome. So, nine A.M. Monday?"

"I will be here."

"Wonderful. And it's up to you, but if you like, bring your swimsuit." Peggy gestured around her. "If this is the California you wanted, you had might as well enjoy it while you can."

After a moment, Laurence smiled. The women said their goodbyes.

Laurence returned Monday morning. She and her employer worked together, opening shipping boxes and creating stacks of papers. In the afternoon Peggy glanced at her watch. "Five o'clock already."

"That was fast." Laurence and Peggy's desks were both covered in papers, folders, binders, labels and more.

"Yeah. Hey. I know I asked you to just handle the French stuff. But you're so good at organization, what would you think about helping me with this whole thing? I think if we both tackle it, together, we can get all the papers into the files soon. Then you can get back to working on the French stuff."

"That is fine. I was thinking actually that this would be the best idea."

"Why didn't you say anything?"

"Because you are the boss." She said it with her lilting French accent: *busssss*.

"Well, stop thinking of me as the boss. Ready for a drink?"

"Yes."

"Me too. I'll change and meet you down there."

When Peggy walked into the pool area in her kimono, she saw Laurence looking away. The French girl turned to her. "This is new?"

A new bar with a Tiki design stood near the pool. It sported a thatched roof with leather stools. Mini-fridges and coolers hummed inside.

"Oh, yeah. I had it built over the weekend." Peggy walked over to it and stepped behind the counter. "Isn't it great!"

"You... said, 'I will build a bar?'"

"Well, have it built. I know a contractor." Peggy scooped ice into a blender. Its din paused the conversation for a moment. "I've been thinking about doing it for a while, and decided, what the hell."

"And… this house does not belong to you?"

"Nope." Peggy frowned, looking under the counter. "I told them specifically to put the salt and margarita mix in here… Ah! Here we go."

"What will the owner say?"

"I called him Friday after you left. I made him an offer he couldn't refuse."

Laurence said nothing. She accepted the margarita that Peggy slid across the counter to her.

"I said," the host continued, "'How about I build you a bar. For free. I'll take pictures of the patio before it goes up. You don't like it, I'll have it put back exactly the way it was when my lease is done.' He said, 'Deal.'" The older woman smiled, made her own drink, and they walked to the chairs by the pool.

"It is a very nice bar," the French girl said.

"Thanks. It doesn't really go with the rest of this place. Early modern, I think this house's style is called. But screw it, I wanted a Tiki bar. Anyway, if the owner or, more likely, his wife decides that they don't like it, I'll just rip it up and take it with me wherever I'm going next. Cheers!"

They toasted. After a sip, Peggy removed her kimono. Her figure threw a curvy shadow. She glanced at the girl. "No swimsuit for you, huh?"

In response, Laurence stood up. Expressionless as always, she removed her T-shirt and shorts, revealing a pretty blue bikini underneath. The French girl's body was slim and athletic, a runner's build, with small breasts. Her freckled peachy-white skin was so pale it almost reflected the sun.

"Aha," Peggy said.

Laurence sat back down. She gazed out at the sand. It was empty. "I have seen a few beaches here, but none as nice as this one." She turned to Peggy. "Why are there no people?"

"It's private. No access to the public."

"Aha."

Over the next few days, a ritual developed. Peggy and Laurence would work all day, with a short break for lunch (provided by YuLing), and at five they would repair to the pool area. Gradually, Peggy began talking more and more about her father.

"He and I would talk on the phone every day. Every day," she repeated. They were sitting in their usual teak chairs by the hot tub.

"That is wonderful, to be so close."

"He tried getting me to come back to Canada. I said, 'Dummy, you should be in Los Angeles!' I called him dummy. He called me idiot."

Laurence's eyebrows rose.

"It's tough, you know." The older woman looked down at her drink. She touched the rim with her finger. "I'm still, like, thinking to myself that I need to tell my dad something when I call him later in the day. And—"

Peggy sobbed suddenly. She dropped her glass; it shattered on the tiles.

Laurence leapt to her feet. She took two steps, careful of the broken shards, and put her hand on her employer's shoulder.

"I'm sorry," Peggy gasped.

"Don't apologize."

"This just happens sometimes." Peggy took a paper napkin and blew her nose. "Ever since he died. I just... sometimes it will all hit me, and I can't control anything. The other night, I started crying in the kitchen, and my legs just gave out. I spent twenty minutes on the floor, weeping like a little girl."

"Perhaps we should not speak of him?"

"No." The older woman wiped her eyes with her hand. "It's healthy to talk about him. I'm just sorry I'm boring you with it."

"You're not boring me. I think he sounds wonderful. Really."

Peggy looked up at Laurence, smiled, and squeezed the girl's hand.

When Laurence stood up to go, Peggy rose also. She walked her to the front door. "So this is... Thursday, right?"

"Yes," the French girl said.

"Only one more day till the weekend."

"You have plans?"

"No. But I need a break from all this crap." She pointed at the upstairs. "You too, probably."

"It is fine."

"Such poise. Are all French girls as classy as you?"

"Of course."

"Good thing you're all over in France, then. Otherwise, chicks like me wouldn't have a chance. Hey. Seriously. Thank you."

Peggy kissed Laurence on both cheeks. Then, on impulse, she hugged the girl. After a moment, Laurence hugged her back.

Finally, they pulled apart. "So, tomorrow, right?" the older woman said.

*"Comme d'habitude."* Laurence smiled—a rare occasion, but becoming less rare—and opened the door. Peggy closed it after her.

The next day, at five o'clock, the women congratulated themselves. Almost all of the papers had been completely filed in Laurence's system. The HON cabinets bulged with documents.

"I do believe it's time for a drink. Or two," Peggy said.

Laurence rose from her desk, looking tired. "Today, two perhaps, yes."

As they prepared to leave, the French girl paused. She pointed. "I have been meaning to ask. What is that?"

Peggy looked. From their high vantage point they could see through the office's window a small platform in the ocean, bobbing gently. It appeared to be between one hundred and two hundred yards out from the shore, just large enough to set a small car upon.

The older woman shrugged. "I don't know. It's a raft of some kind. I guess it's anchored to the bottom. It's been there ever since I rented this place, last year."

"You have never seen anyone on it?"

"No. Why?"

Laurence stared at the raft. "This is a mysterious thing. Why is it there?"

"I can ask around, if you like."

The girl shrugged.

"Ready for that drink?"

"Very much."

Out by the pool, after Peggy had prepared their Manhattans and margaritas, she and Laurence settled into their chairs as usual. YuLing arrived to say good-bye, then departed.

"She's leaving early today," Peggy remarked. "Her son is getting married."

"Oh, yes?"

"Yeah."

"You are attending the wedding?"

"No way. I hate weddings. I even hated my own, when it happened. But I gave the newlyweds a nice wedding present. I'm sure they won't mind that I won't be there. They don't know me, anyway."

The French girl considered her employer. "You say: you hated your wedding?"

"Oh yeah."

"Why?" Laurence began applying tanning

lotion to her skin. Her *peau* had begun to brown from days in the afternoon sun.

"My wedding…" Peggy said. She paused. "My dad gave great advice. He was the sharpest, shrewdest man I've ever known. But do you know what the best advice he ever gave me was?"

"'Don't get married?'"

Peggy laughed loud and long. "No. He was over the moon about that. But he insisted that I make Jeremy—my fiancé—sign a prenup." She ran a finger down the outside of her drink. Condensation dripped onto the tiled patio. "I almost hated my dad for doing that. Can you imagine how awkward that conversation was that I had with Jeremy? 'Honey, I love you so much, we're going to be so happy together, now please just sign on the dotted line.'"

Laurence made a face. "Could you have said no?"

"Yeah. And I came close. Really close. But something in the back of my mind told me that my dad was right. As it turned out, he was. I don't think Jeremy was actually after my money when we were married, but our divorce… it was the most vicious, brutal thing I've ever experienced. The venom was unbelievable. I had caught him cheating on me, and the first thing I did was send an email to his mother and father and all of his family, telling them exactly who he had been cheating with and the means by which he deceived me—his lies, his phony phone calls, everything."

"Oh, no."

"I was hurt. And you know what? I'm still not sorry." She waited a beat, then: "He screamed about how I was going to BE sorry, that he was going to take everything I had." Peggy gave Laurence a slow shrewd grin. "No he did-ennnnt," she sang in a singsong voice. Laughing, she toasted the sky. "Thank you, daddy!"

Laurence smiled, then offered her glass. Peggy clinked it with her own.

"I think," the French girl began, "if I said to my fiancé, 'Sign a prenuptial agreement please,' his signature would be on the paper before I had even finished speaking. He is rich, and I have nothing. So!" Laurence made a gesture and flipped her head; but she winced, setting her drink down abruptly upon the table between them.

Peggy sat up. "Are you all right?"

"I have a, thing, here." Laurence raised her left hand up and across her body to massage where her neck and shoulder met.

"No wonder. You were bent over your desk all day. All week. Here." Peggy rose from her chair and walked around. Laying gentle hands on Laurence's shoulders, she began to rub.

The French girl dropped her own hand. "Thank you," she sighed.

"Holy crimoley. Your shoulders feel like rocks. Especially the right one."

"Yes." The girl closed her eyes, tilting her head. "I feel stress easily. I have had two ulcers, and I am not yet twenty-five."

Peggy gaped at the back of the girl's head as she massaged. "Listen. Don't stress about this job. I'm going to be fine. And you are doing perfect. It's nothing to worry about."

Laurence did not answer. She seemed to be lost in a zone.

After kneading the girl's shoulders and neck for a long time, the older woman finally released her. "There! I think I got most of that knot out."

It took Laurence a few seconds to reply. "That was so nice," she murmured. Her eyes opened. She slid a finger under her bikini top's strap and stared at Peggy. "Are you... have you been, professional?"

The older woman smiled. "I've had training. I'll tell you about it some time. But didn't you say you needed to leave by seven?"

"Oh. Yes." She glanced up. The sky had grown dark.

"It's already five past."

"The hostel closes the doors at eight." Laurence rose. "Thank you."

"I'll walk you out."

At the door, Laurence leaned in and gave Peggy a two-cheek kiss.

"You beat me to it," the older woman said. She laughed.

"I must run to the bus. But I will see you,

Monday, early."

"Better."

They traded a long smile. Then the girl left.

At the end of their working day on Monday, Peggy and Laurence assessed what they had accomplished: all of the papers were neatly filed away, and the French girl had indexed important information in a spreadsheet that she, much to the older woman's amazement, found a way to share between their computers.

"It is called Google documents," Laurence said. "Log in and you will see everything. You can change everything as well."

After following the girl's instructions, the older woman shook her head in wonder. "I can't believe it. I think I'm actually going to be ready."

"As long as no more boxes arrive from Ottawa."

"Let's hope." Peggy glanced at an empty DHL Shipping box on the floor. "The last one came four days ago, so hopefully that's it." She yawned. "It's just after five. Ready?"

"Yes."

As the bikini-clad women settled into their chairs holding drinks, Laurence shot Peggy a quizzical glance. "You said, last time, you have training? For the massage?"

"Oh. Yeah." Peggy adjusted her custom bikini's top, flipped her hair over her shoulders, and settled back. She took a big sip of her drink, draining half of it. She looked prosperous and sexy, a magazine cover waiting for a photographer. "When I was younger, I had some romantic ideas about work." Peggy explained that she had followed an ambition to become a great masseuse. She had spent years training in Japan and Sweden.

"And... then?" The French girl regarded her with wide eyes, as if more impressed by this than by anything else she had seen or heard at Peggy's home.

"Then I got a job in Los Angeles at a spa." Peggy took another gulp of her drink, draining it. "I lasted two weeks."

"What happened?"

"Rich old crabby ladies. And dirty old men who stared at my chest. That's what happened." Peggy looked down, touching her stomach absently. "I realized I really liked massage, I loved it even, but I didn't enjoy doing it for strangers. Especially rude and creepy people."

Laurence nodded. Then she smiled, offering Peggy a coquettish glance. "You give me one, again?"

Peggy rolled her eyes.

"I have been working so hard," Laurence whined. "Bent over the desk. Working on your documents." She looked under her eyebrows at her employer, making a sad face.

"Sure, guilt me out," Peggy muttered. She was unable to suppress a smile. "You found the weakness of Jewish princesses."

Laurence beamed. She rose and moved her chair so that it was just in front of Peggy's, facing away. The girl sat lightly upon it once more, pulling her hair away and over to offer her neck and shoulders.

"I can see this is going to be a thing," Peggy said. She laid her hands upon the girl's skin and her fingertips pressed, searched for tightness.

"Wait," Laurence said. Peggy lifted her palms. Laurence bent forward, undid her bikini top with a quick movement, and tossed it onto the table. She leaned back again.

After a pause, the French girl looked over her shoulder at Peggy. "Problem?"

"Sure you want to go topless?" the older woman asked.

"It does not bother me. In Europe…"

"Yeah, I know. In Europe everybody does it. But here, you can get arrested."

Laurence stared. "By who?"

"Well, the cops, if they catch you…"

"But this is a private beach. I have seen no cops here."

"There's also the neighbors. You want them looking?"

Laurence glanced to her right. "Who lives there?" She pointed at a large dark adjacent structure that looked like the ultimate '70s beach house. The window blinds were drawn, shutting out the sun.

"An elderly couple. I don't know their names."

The girl looked to her left. Another large dwelling, styled like a Mediterranean villa. "And there?"

"No one. I think. The owner's absent."

Laurence looked back over her shoulder at Peggy. "I think no one will notice, and if they do I do not care. But if YOU care..." She reached for her top.

"Whoa!" Peggy held up her palms. "If you're happy, I'm happy. Just giving you the heads-up."

"The what?"

"A cultural context."

"Ah." The girl smiled, leaning back again. Her top remained on the table. "Thank you for this context."

Peggy resumed massaging. The girl's shoulders were tight, though not as bad as on the past Friday. Her eyes closed again. She exhaled, a sound of pleasure.

"I can see this is going to be a thing," the older woman repeated.

Laurence's eyelids opened, slowly. She looked drowsy. "Did you buy that in Japan?" She nodded at the kimono that Peggy always wore to the pool. It lay in a heap on the tiles where she had let it drop.

"Yep." The brunette shifted slightly in her seat, giving herself more leverage. "Like it?"

Laurence did not reply. Peggy glanced. The girl's eyes were closed again, savoring her masseuse's expert kneading. A tiny moan escaped her lips.

Peggy looked at the small strips of white flesh on the shoulders where Laurence's bikini straps had rested. Peggy's gaze wandered further. The French girl's breasts pointed straight at the late-afternoon sun like spears. They shone almost porcelain-white, speckled with freckles and capped with delicate pink nipples.

After staring at them for a few minutes, Peggy started, catching herself. "Your boobs are gonna burn," she said. "We're facing into the sun."

Laurence groaned. Like a petulant child, she grabbed a tube of suntan lotion off the table and squirted goo into a palm. The blonde rubbed her hands together and slapped lotion onto her breasts with an impatient roughness before settling back into her chair.

As Peggy continued to work the shoulder and neck muscles through Laurence's damp skin, the older woman looked down once more. A glob of white lotion rested on the girl's breast. After a while, it began to slowly slide down. Peggy watched it finally drop off. It landed on the girl's bare thigh.

At length, Peggy gave Laurence's shoulders one last squeeze and lifted her hands. "All right, French girl. How do you say 'That's it?'"

Laurence pouted and protested, but Peggy held firm.

The next day, as Laurence walked up to the bar, she pulled off her tight T-shirt with a fluid movement. "The ocean is so beautiful today," she called back to Peggy. Gazing at the water, the French girl reached with both hands and unclipped her bra. She set it on the barstool where she had already deposited her shirt.

"Yeah," her employer replied. She passed Laurence and walked around behind the bar to make the drinks as usual, trying not to glance. Laurence unzipped her jeans and removed them. She sat her bikini-covered bottom on a free barstool.

"C'est magnifique," the girl murmured. A storm during the previous night had removed the usual layer of smog upon the horizon, creating a golden glow all over the ocean's water. Laurence kept her eyes upon it, not even glancing as Peggy slid her customary margarita across the bar counter to her.

"It's nice, that's for sure," the older woman said. She seemed preoccupied. "I think I may need a third drink today, so I'm going to make it right now, okay? Here in the states, we call that 'triple fisting.'"

Laurence finally gave her employer her full attention. "What is wrong?"

"I dunno, just a little stressed. It's fine." Peggy crushed three times her usual amount of ice in the blender.

"Do you want me to help you again with the files?" This had been the first day that Laurence had returned full-time to working on only the

French documents.

"No, I'm fine. Just distracted. Say," the brunette said, changing the subject. She twisted suddenly to point at the waves, making her heavy breasts wobble in their bikini top. "Do you surf?"

"No."

"Well, I was going to say, there is a surfboard in the garage."

"I love to swim. I love the ocean."

Peggy lifted her drinks, and they walked to their usual chairs. "Well, feel free," the older woman said. "But there is no lifeguard, and you can't depend on me to save you. Even if I do have these life preservers built in." She shook her bosom playfully. Then she shivered. "The ocean scares me to death."

"Why?" They sat.

"I saw *Jaws* when I was a kid."

"Ah."

"I'm terrified of the ocean. I won't even dip my toes in."

"Pfff."

"Seriously. But, if you want to take a dip, be my guest."

Laurence looked out at the water. "Have you ever swam in the dark?" she asked in her soft, lilting French accent.

"Night swimming?"

"Yes."

"In the ocean?" Peggy looked at the waves disbelievingly.

"Yes."

"It sounds like a good way to die. And die screaming. I don't even know what kind of currents are out there."

"You have these... how do you call them?" The girl pointed far down the beach. At a distant point, only just visible, was an outcropping of boulders that stuck into the sea like a giant finger.

"Breakwaters."

"Yes."

"I'm still not jumping into the sea. And I don't think you should, either. Swimming at night? You could get lost."

Laurence closed her eyes. She tilted her head, letting the sun warm it. "You can know from the noise of the waves where the beach is. And here there are many high buildings with lights. In moonlight, I think it is absolutely no problem."

Peggy just shook her head.

Soon, the French girl requested what she called "the daily massage." After token resistance, Peggy nodded. The smiling blonde moved her chair in front of Peggy as before. Once she was situated, the older woman pulled her own chair up slightly so that her splayed knees touched the back of the girl's chair. Peggy placed her hands on Laurence's shoulders and began rubbing.

"So tell me about this guy, back in France. Your to-be husband."

"His name is Phillipe."

"Whoa."

"What?"

"You just felt… you got tense, all of a sudden. Relax."

"I am fine."

The older woman slowly worked her hands from the outside of Laurence's shoulders up, ending at her ears. She rubbed the earlobes gently. The girl sighed, and her eyes closed.

"That's better. You're loosening up," Peggy said.

"You are… you have amazing skill."

"Yeah, yeah. Flatterer. You're just trying to get more massages."

"Even if I was, that would be also a compliment, no?" The girl moaned softly.

"So, Phillipe. What does he do?"

"He owns a business in Paris. He repossesses airplanes. Small ones. People buy them, and when they cannot pay the bank…"

"Right. You're getting tense again. Stop it."

"Sorry." She sighed.

"Do you not want to talk about him?"

"No, I mean yes, I like talking about him. We have been apart for a long time, perhaps this is why I am tense."

"Gotcha."

"He is very successful."

"How did you meet?"

"After I finished my business degree, I interviewed for a job at his company. At the end he said, 'I cannot offer you employment, but I can offer you dinner.'"

Peggy made a repulsed face. "Wow."

"What?" The girl's eyes opened. She looked at Peggy over her shoulder.

"That's kind of sexual harassment, or something, in this country."

"Even if the man has not employed you?"

"It's sort of out of bounds."

"I see." Laurence turned forward again and craned her head to give Peggy better access to the base of her neck. "I think, and I do not mean to be rude, but things are different in France."

"That's what they tell me." Peggy laughed. "So... you haven't known him very long?"

"No," the French girl said sharply. "I mean no," she added in a gentler voice. "It has been, I think you say, a 'whirlwind romance.'"

Laurence had again tensed visibly. Peggy asked no more questions. The older woman worked to loosen the girl's upper-body muscles once more. After a while, she succeeded. Eyes closed, Laurence sighed and smiled.

After many minutes, the girl's eyelids opened slightly. Glancing over her shoulder she watched a moment, then smiled. "They cannot compare."

"What?" Peggy asked, startled. Laurence had caught her staring at her breasts.

"These." The blonde shook her chest playfully; her small breasts wobbled only a little. "They cannot compare to yours."

"I think you've had your massage ration for

the day," the older woman said, pretending to be stern. She lifted her hands.

Once again Laurence pouted and protested, and once again Peggy held firm. Finally, the girl shrugged. She looked out at the ocean again. "What time is it?"

Glancing at her phone, Peggy answered: "About six-thirty."

"I would like to swim." The girl rose. She looked at her host. "Will you come with me?"

"I can watch you from here."

"Okay."

Laurence turned and walked toward steps that led to the sand.

"Remember," Peggy warned, "you don't want to get caught topless."

The French girl smiled back at her, not breaking stride. Taking the stairs two at a time, she hit the beach running. Peggy watched her grow smaller as she sprinted toward the ocean. As she reached the water the foam from a large wave rushed and eddied around her feet; she dashed forward, pulling her knees high with every step. A wave arrived to greet her and she jackknifed into it.

Peggy stood up. She shielded her brow against the remains of the dying sun shining in her eyes. As seconds passed, she appeared more anxious. Finally, she turned and followed Laurence's path down onto the sand and toward the water.

At the edge of the surf, Peggy stopped. She

looked around uneasily. After a short time, she appeared like she was ready to start shouting for help.

Laurence's head popped out of the churning ocean's surface, silhouetted by the setting sun. Peggy exhaled. The girl approached, rising slowly out of the water.

"Aren't you cold?" The older woman asked when she had finally arrived.

Laurence laughed and said no. She flicked her head from side to side, ejecting water from her ears. She seemed vibrant, happy, alive. "After you enter, for two seconds you are cold, then it leaves you."

"You were in there forever." They began walking back to the house.

"Yes?" Laurence appeared puzzled. "I thought I swam only a short time. I'm sorry. I did not want to worry you."

Peggy entered the house to find a towel. When she returned, she saw the French girl rinsing off in the outside shower. Her bikini bottoms lay in a soggy heap next to the shower's drain. The French girl's body showed very little fat, yet boasted tight curves. A thin blonde bush created a small triangle between her legs.

Peggy placed the folded towel on the chair nearest to the girl. Laurence opened her eyes and smiled. "Hello!"

"Hello."

Laurence turned to shut off the water. Peggy's

eyes glanced at the girl's pert butt, round and tanlined.

After a quick dry-off, Laurence pulled on her jeans, commando. "A wonderful day."

Peggy smiled. "I haven't seen you this happy since we opened those first boxes of documents."

The girl laughed. "This is a joke, right?"

Peggy nodded.

"It is so good to swim in the ocean. Even if it is not quite dark." Laurence walked to the barstools. "There's nothing else that makes you feel so alive." She donned her bra, fastening it behind her. "You feel free."

"Uh-huh," Peggy said, watching.

"I cannot explain it." The blonde put on her T-shirt, pulling her wet hair out and tying it into a knot behind her head. "You must experience it to understand. Will you come with me, next time?"

"Hell no."

Laurence laughed again. Nothing could sour her mood. She twisted water out of her bikini bottoms and shoved them into her jeans pocket.

At the door, Laurence grew serious. "You do not mind, the massage?"

"Of course not. I'll just take it out of your paycheck."

"This is another joke, I hope."

"Sure. Although you wouldn't believe what my rate was, for those two weeks I worked at the spa. But really, don't worry. It's nice to be appreciated."

A dreamy look came over the girl's face. "I have always loved massage, the receiving. If I was wealthy, I would not spend money on food, or even wine. Only massage. Every day, all day."

"Yeah, well. I have a feeling the poor girl or dude might get tired."

Laurence laughed again. She looked very pretty.

"I'm really glad you had such a great time," Peggy continued. "You need to relax more. You always seem kind of serious and stressed."

"Ah yes. Massage plus swimming always gives me the perfect day." She kissed Peggy slowly on both cheeks. "Have a good weekend."

Peggy flushed. "Okay, uh. So, today's Thursday. The weekend's not quite here yet."

Laurence slapped her forehead. "I forgot!"

"That's okay." Peggy considered a wet spot on the girl's jeans where her pocket held the bikini bottom. "You want a bag or something for that?"

"This? No, it is not necessary. I will see you tomorrow."

"Bright and early," Peggy said, beaming as she opened the door. Laurence's happiness was infectious.

"Bright and early," the girl repeated. She bounded out, waving to Peggy over her shoulder.

Later that night, in bed, Peggy glanced up from a book. Her phone on her bedside table was buzzing. She set the book down and picked up the phone. The caller ID said, "UNKNOWN."

She waited. Shortly after it stopped ringing, the voicemail light appeared. She called her voicemail and entered her security code.

"Hello Peggy." It was Laurence. She sounded as clinical and detached as she had been the first day they had met. "This is the number I have for you from the temp agency paperwork. I hope you receive this message. I am sorry to say that I have sad news from home. My father has died."

Peggy's jaw dropped. "So," Laurence continued, "I will not be arriving for work tomorrow. I'm very sorry. I will give you information about when I may return, if you still want me, later. Please accept my apologies. Due to the nature of this emergency, I cannot anticipate when I will have more firm information to tell you. Bye."

Peggy dialed the number. She received a recording saying that that number did not receive incoming calls.

As she was finishing dressing, her phone rang again. "UNKNOWN."

Peggy answered immediately. "Laurence?"

"Hello." The girl's voice sounded as flat as before.

"Jesus, honey. I'm so sorry."

"Thank you. I will be at work tomorrow, after all."

"What?"

"That is why I'm calling. Before, I called you too soon. I cannot return in time for the funeral.

So I will remain here in California."

"You can't... wait a minute. Where are you?"

"At the hostel."

"Do you have any other phone, besides the one you're calling on?"

"No. It is the house phone. It does not accept incoming calls, that is why I did not leave the number..."

"Yeah," Peggy interrupted. "I found that out. Just tell me, from the beginning, what happened."

Laurence's father had journeyed to Marseille on business. The girl had not known that, but then she knew very little about his life. Soon after he arrived in that city, he came down with pneumonia and entered the hospital. After ten days, he succumbed. His passing had happened almost a week ago. Her stepmother had not bothered to inform Laurence. Laurence had only discovered what had happened from an email sent from a hospital administration person, who when filing the necessary paperwork had noticed her name and email address on the hospital form her father had filled out on admission. He had listed Laurence as his number-two next of kin, following his wife.

"Oh my God," Peggy said.

"After I called you, I called Michelle—his wife. She told me the funeral is scheduled for tomorrow. So I cannot return in time."

A long pause followed. "Peggy?"

"Hold on, I'm thinking." Another pause.

When she spoke again, a new tone had entered her voice—strong and hard. "Will the funeral be in Toulouse?"

"Yes."

"What time tomorrow?"

Laurence told her.

"You know where?"

"Michelle told me where. Why?"

"Since I can't call you, you call me back in fifteen minutes. Okay?"

"Peggy, thank you, but—"

"No time. Call me back. Bye."

Fifteen minutes later, at the youth hostel, Laurence walked to the phone in the common area and dialed Peggy. Peggy picked up on the first ring.

"Where are you?" she asked.

"Sorry?"

"What's your address. Where is your hostel?" Laurence heard the sound of a car's engine revving high.

The French girl told her. "But why…"

"You're on a flight to Toulouse, with a connection in Paris." A squealing noise as tires spun over pavement. "But there's a catch."

"What? What catch?"

"We have to get to the airport in less than an hour. Okay, what's the cross-street of this hostel?"

Laurence told her.

"Go get your passport and anything else you

need, but be outside in two minutes." Peggy hung up.

As they raced toward LAX in Peggy's shiny Mercedes convertible, Laurence tried to hand her employer's phone back to Peggy.

"Leave it on your seat," the brunette said. She accelerated, flying through a yellow light.

"My aunt says she will meet me at the Toulouse airport. If I arrive."

"Good. Okay, so when you get to the LAX gate, show them your passport. They'll give you your tickets."

"I will run."

"You better."

As the car screeched to a stop in front of startled baggage handlers, Laurence threw open her passenger door. She turned back to Peggy. "Thank you." She kissed Peggy on both cheeks, squeezed her hand, then dashed into the terminal.

Two days later, at lunch time, Peggy's phone rang. She set down her fork and answered the call. "Hello?"

"Hello Peggy."

"Hi." A pause. "How are you?"

"I'm fine." The girl's voice was as calm as ever. "I will be returning tomorrow, so I will be at work in the afternoon."

"Never mind that. God, honey. What's happening? Did you make the funeral?"

"Yes. I will tell you more when I return. My phone here, it is the long distance."

"Oh."

"But I wanted to say thank you, and that I would be returning tomorrow."

"You know, the return flight on that tickets is flexible. If you want to stay longer, you can. Really, don't worry about me. Just take care of yourself."

"I am fine. I am ready to return."

"Okay, then."

Laurence gave Peggy her flight arrival information.

"So, see you tomorrow!" Peggy concluded, trying to sound upbeat. "I'll pick you up outside Arrivals at the curb."

"Thank you again Peggy." A slight tremor caught the girl's voice. "Goodbye."

"Bye."

The following morning, Peggy's Mercedes slowed to a stop outside the international arrivals pickup area of LAX. Laurence was waiting, in the same clothes she had worn when she left. The only difference was that she was now wearing sunglasses.

The girl opened the Mercedes passenger door and entered. "Hello." She shut the door after her.

"Hi!" Peggy drove away, watching for speeding cars and shuttle buses.

"Thank you for getting me. And for the flight. For everything." Laurence removed her sunglasses. Her eyes were red-rimmed.

"Stop thanking me. Listen, I need to figure out

how to get back on the freeway, so just give me a minute and then we can talk."

"Of course."

After Peggy had negotiated the spaghetti of roads and lanes surrounding LAX and had set the car back on a course to Malibu, she exhaled. Turning to Laurence, she opened her mouth to speak.

The French girl was asleep, collapsed against the car door. She looked utterly exhausted.

Her employer paused, then gently reached across her to lock her car door.

When they finally rolled into Peggy's garage, Laurence stirred.

"Hey, sleepyhead." The older woman tousled the girl's hair.

Laurence blinked. "Where are we?"

"Home. Come on, there's a surprise waiting for you." Peggy unclipped her seatbelt and exited the car. Laurence followed her.

In the kitchen, YuLing beamed. "Welcome!"

The housekeeper stood before a set table. A bowl of scallops and mushrooms in cream sauce sat in the middle with a side of steamed green beans. Bread rolls flanked the plates.

Peggy smiled. "I asked YuLing if she could make some Coquilles Saint-Jacques. And haricots… verts? That's green beans, right?"

Laurence looked at the table wonderingly. Then she turned to Peggy, a question on her face.

Peggy shrugged. "It was the most French meal

I could think of."

The girl laughed. It seemed like an accumulation of stress fell from her. She stood up straighter, and touched her hair. "You're very kind."

"Well, let's eat! Although, can you believe it, I forgot the wine."

"No problem. I think if I drink anything, anyway, I will fall down."

After lunch, Laurence dabbed her mouth daintily with a napkin. "That was wonderful. Better than in France, even."

"You shouldn't lie to your employer."

Laurence looked hurt.

"Oh. Okay," Peggy added. A pause. "It was all YuLing. You can thank her."

"I will. But this was your idea, no?"

Peggy nodded.

"So I will thank you, also." Laurence smiled, with difficulty. She looked like she had not smiled in a while.

"Do you want to take a nap?"

The girl shook her head, making her blonde hair slide over her shoulders. "I want to work."

"Really?"

"Yes. It will help me to do something with my mind that is not all of… that." She waved, vaguely, indicating something behind her.

"Then you got it. Come on."

Laurence worked more intensely than ever before, organizing French documents and making notes in many separate spreadsheets. She showed Peggy her calculations.

"These three companies have no valuation statements," the girl muttered, leaning over Peggy's desk and showing her a printout. "I will call them, and ask they send the proper documentation."

Peggy nodded. "With the time difference, the offices are closed now. But you can try them in the morning."

"It is inexcusable," Laurence said. "These people! If they do not provide the information, they are stupid, or corrupt. Either way—"

"Okay, okay." Peggy studied Laurence carefully. "You'll figure it out in the morning. Calm down."

The girl sighed. She nodded, rubbing her eyes.

"Ready for a drink?"

"Very much."

"Wait: you said earlier that if you drank, you would fall down."

"I'm feeling better. Thank you." Laurence looked at Peggy with warm eyes. The older woman smiled back. They walked out of the office.

At the bar, as Peggy set aside her own drinks, Laurence said: "I think today I will have two, also."

In moments the brunette slid two margaritas across the counter to Laurence. The women walked to their chairs.

"It's overcast today." Peggy looked up and adjusted her bikini.

Laurence pulled off her T-shirt and removed her bra, as usual. Unbuttoning her jeans, she paused.

"What?"

"My swimsuit. It is at the hostel." She sighed, a long exasperated sound. Finally she shrugged and pushed her jeans off her legs. Her panties were plain white cotton.

"Keep going," Peggy deadpanned. "They're shooting a Girls Gone Wild special later."

"A girls what?"

"Nothing."

"It is so good to be back here." Laurence raised one of her drinks to her lips and tipped it, draining the glass.

"You'll have a good time anywhere, drinking like that." Peggy smiled.

The girl looked at her. "Can I request something?" she asked in a serious tone.

"Sure."

"I do not wish yet to discuss my trip. It is… raw."

"I completely understand."

"Raw is the right word?"

"Absolutely."

Laurence nodded. She settled back in her chair, closing her eyes and letting the sun warm her face.

After a few minutes had passed, she suddenly

opened her eyes again and thrust her hand forward to gulp down her second drink.

Startled, Peggy asked: "Are you okay?"

"Yes." The girl touched a drop of liquid on her lips. "My mind is just..." she struggled, then shrugged. "Difficult to control. Too many things."

"I understand, but... never mind. Can I help?"

Laurence sighed and began to shake her head. But then she stopped and gave her employer a sideways smirk.

"What?"

In response, Laurence rose and walked to a lounge chair. She lowered its backrest so that the surface was completely horizontal. The blonde pirouetted gracefully and laid on her stomach, smiling back over her shoulder at Peggy.

"Huh? I don't get it."

Laurence rubbed her shoulder, raising her eyebrows.

"Oh, God," the older woman groaned with false exasperation. "So that's where we're at, now? You want the full treatment?"

The girl kept rubbing her shoulder and smiling in an oh-so-cute way.

Peggy rose. "How do you say 'spoiled brat' in French?"

"*Belle fille.*'"

"That means pretty girl."

Laurence laughed, turning her face away. She raised her feet up and made a happy quick scissoring motion.

The older woman picked up a towel and folded it carefully. "Most massage tables are waist-high, you know. You owe me extra for this one."

The girl did not reply, only paddling her feet faster.

Stooping, Peggy set the folded towel on the titles next to Laurence before kneeling upon the soft surface. She placed her hands on the girl's shoulders and squeezed.

"Uuuuhhhhh," the blonde groaned.

"Too hard?"

"No. Please, harder."

Peggy tightened her grip. Laurence made another low noise of pleasure. Her feet fluttered back down.

Peggy worked her way from the neck and shoulders to the girl's back, kneading and pushing, working her fingers. "I'm out of practice. My hands used to be a lot stronger. This particular style is shiatsu, by the way."

"Shiatsu," Laurence said dreamily. "I love shiatsu."

Peggy's hands moved down further. She glanced. The girl's panties were spread elegantly across her cheeks.

"Mmmmm," the girl moaned.

"You want legs too?"

"Yes. And feet? Please?"

"Wow. Way to push it," Peggy said. She

grinned. When the masseuse's hands reached the waistband of Laurence's panties, they rose and moved over the round rump to descend upon the upper thighs.

The girl mumbled something in French.

Peggy, focused on her work, asked: "What?"

Laurence did not reply. Peggy kept massaging, rubbing, sliding her hands over the girl's legs. She circled the thighs with her fingers. The older woman's eyes wandered to the girl's butt again. It was a perfect heart shape, moving ever so slightly with the girl's breathing.

Peggy worked her way down the legs, taking her time. Squeezing the girl's knees only lightly, she continued along the calf muscles, running and sliding the heel of her hand up and down. After paying close attention to the ankles with a slipping motion of her thumb and forefinger, she pulled up one of Laurence's feet and shifted her own body. But something in the girl's reaction made her pause. She looked back at her head.

Laurence was asleep. Her light snoring blended with the ocean's distant noise.

Peggy set the foot back down. She slid her hands lightly up the girl's legs. Laurence was dead to the world.

As Peggy's fingers arrived at the area where legs met buttocks, the woman hesitated. She stared again at the girl's rump. A hint of tanline could be seen where the panties' hem rode up slightly. The blonde's ass was perfectly soft and full, blooming with the promise of a pretty girl's youth.

At length, the older woman sighed. She patted the girl's butt, letting her hand linger for just a second upon the white cotton. Then she stood up.

\* \* \*

Laurence's eyes opened. It was dark. She lifted her shoulders with a jerk, making one of the two towels that covered her slide off. "Peggy?"

"Over here."

The girl turned her head. Peggy sat close by, still wearing her bikini. She inserted a bookmark into a paperback and closed it. Her book light glowed in the dark, illuminating her face.

Laurence gaped, tilting her face up to the black sky. "How long have I been sleeping?"

"A while. I didn't want to disturb you. You needed your rest."

"What is the time?"

"A little after ten."

The girl's eyes opened wide. "My hostel is closed. I am too late!"

"Yeah, I know. You can sleep here. I was actually about to wake you anyway. Perfect timing. It'll be getting chilly soon."

"Sleep here?"

"Yeah. If that's all right?"

"It is fine, of course." Laurence stifled a yawn. "But you have done so much for me already."

"Like I said, I'll send you a bill." Peggy grinned. "You hungry?"

The girl shook her head.

"Okay. Come on, let's turn in. We have a big day tomorrow. I think I'm finally getting a handle on all those spreadsheets you made."

Peggy stood up and switched off her book light. Laurence rose and gathered her shirt and jeans. Then she followed her employer into the house.

On the second floor, Peggy stopped and turned around. She pointed to an open room with a bed. "Guest quarters."

Laurence glanced and nodded.

"It has its own bathroom. There's sheets and towels. And a bathrobe in one of the drawers somewhere."

Laurence smiled. "It is as nice as your kimono?"

"Uh, that would be a no. Okay. How long have you been wearing those clothes?"

The girl glanced at the bundle in her hand. "Since the day, I think, you took me to the airport."

"That's what I was afraid of. Give them to me. I'll throw them in the washing machine."

Laurence retrieved a few items from the pockets, then handed the jeans over to Peggy along with her T-shirt. Then she slipped her panties down, stepped out of them, and dropped them upon the pile her host held.

Laurence stood nude on the carpet. A few seconds passed. "All righty, then," Peggy said for lack of anything else.

In response, Laurence stepped forward and embraced her, holding her close. Peggy remained motionless. After a long moment, Peggy repeated: "All righty, then."

"Thank you," Laurence whispered. The naked girl kissed Peggy on her cheek. After looking into her eyes, the blonde touched the older woman's face. Then she entered her guest room, closing the door softly behind her.

Peggy remained standing in the hall a long time. Then she turned to descend the stairs to the garage, where the washing machine was.

Many hours later, Laurence awoke in bed. She stretched like a cat, yawned, and opened her eyes. Weak sunlight streamed through the window.

She heard a sound and made a puzzled face. A machine nearby was humming and a distinct *thump-thump-thump* could be heard from the same direction.

Rising, the naked girl searched a few drawers before discovering a bathrobe. She donned it, tied the cloth belt around her waist, and exited the room.

Down the hall, she found the source of the noise. Peggy was running on a treadmill. An iPad attached to the console played a show from the E Network. Peggy watched, listening on headphones. Sweat ran down her body. She wore a tight lycra tank top, which was of course clearly custom made. Her big breasts, held perfectly close to her body, did not wobble at all. Spandex tights hugged the toned curvy lower half of her body. Glancing at the door, she smiled and removed her earbuds. "Hi!"

Laurence smiled back. "Hi."

"Sorry, did I wake you?"

"No, it is fine. My sleep was perfect."

"Good. Hey, before I started running I put your clothes in the dryer. They should be done by now. You know where the dryer is?"

"In the garage?"

"Yep."

"I will get them. Should I wait in the kitchen?"

"Wait wherever you like. YuLing should be here in a few minutes. Just tell her what you want for breakfast. I'll be down shortly."

They smiled at each other. Laurence departed.

Later, in the office, Peggy tapped her computer's screen with a pencil. "I think I'm having a revelation."

Laurence turned from her papers to look at her. "What?"

"Unless I'm very mistaken, the Oil Sands stuff in Alberta is worth more than everything else put together."

The French girl nodded. "I still need to get valuations from two companies in Québec province. But yes, from the documents I have seen, I have suspected the same."

"My father liked to invest. In everything. He hated keeping UP with the investments, but anyway. I don't think he really knew what he had, here."

"He was disorganized, you said?"

"Yes… and he didn't listen to anybody. Least of all whatever secretary he had that week. They would always quit, they couldn't take him. So he had piles of papers, towers of them, all over his office." She turned to Laurence with wide eyes. "My father was a wealthy man, as you probably guessed. But if he had realized that his investment in the Oil Sands had taken off… he would have bought an island, or something. He had gone to the next level, and he didn't even know it."

Laurence smiled. "So now you, too, are at the next level?"

"It sure seems that way."

The girl bounded up from her chair and ran to give her startled employer a hug. *"Félicitations!"* she exclaimed. "That means congratulations."

"Oh. Merci!" They laughed.

That afternoon, the women lounged in their usual chairs by the pool. Laurence wore only her panties, as she had the day before.

Peggy sighed. "You know? I think I'm over the hump with all this estate stuff."

Laurence lifted one of two margaritas in front of her. She sipped. "What is, 'hump?'"

"Like, a hill, or obstacle."

"Also, 'fuck,' yes?

"Uh, well, yeah, but I didn't... What I meant was, I think I'm getting a handle on everything. I'm starting to understand exactly what all the pieces of the estate are." That day they had placed a large map of Canada on the wall and indicated the locations of businesses with labeled push-pins. "The meeting with my siblings is in two weeks. By then I should have a really good grasp of the estate. Holy shit though, what a journey, huh? How many hundreds of documents were there?"

"Thousands." The girl closed her eyes and let the sun warm her face.

"I can't believe we did it. Hey. I'm going to need you here when I'm in Ottawa. I'm sure a lot of horse-trading will go down and I'll need you to check facts for me. Can you stay here for a few days while I'm gone? I might need to call at any time."

"Of course." The girl still did not open her eyes.

After a pause, Peggy said: "Anyway. Enough business! You ready for your rub?"

Laurence shielded her face from the sun and glanced sideways. A slow smile. "I was thinking, perhaps something else."

"You're kidding. The way you like massages?"

"Yes. As a way of saying congratulations for today, and thank you, and all of that, I was thinking maybe I can try the massage of you. Massage for you? How do you say that?"

"Uh, just, um, I don't know. I mean, I don't know how you would say that, exactly. But if you want to, sure. You don't have to."

Laurence rose to her feet with a coltish leap. "Of course I do not have to! But I want to." A thought occurred to her. She looked troubled. "And also of course, I have had no training so mine will not be as good as yours…"

Peggy put her at ease. Soon the older woman was face down on the lounge chair with her head lying on crossed forearms. She stretched her toes back as far as they would go, lengthening her prone body.

"So in fact, not only have I no training, I have never even done this before." The blonde girl set a folded towel carefully on the tiles, then knelt upon it.

"How exciting."

"Do not joke, I am nervous. You must tell me how to do this."

Peggy shrugged and closed her eyes. "Just relax. Start high, and work your way down."

"No other advice?"

"Nope. Don't worry. You'll do fine."

Laurence's brow furrowed. She placed her hands upon Peggy's upper back and squeezed gently.

"See there?" Peggy sighed. "You've got the hang of it already."

"This is good?"

"Oh yeah."

More confident, Laurence kneaded Peggy's tanned shoulders, moving inwards towards the neck.

Peggy's smile broadened as the minutes passed. Laurence rubbed down her back slowly, pushing with her fingers, searching for tightness. She reached the strap of Peggy's bikini top.

"I can remove this?"

"Okay, why not," Peggy said after a pause.

The girl unclipped the top and let the straps dangle down on either side of the chair. She moved her hands up and down the length of Peggy's back, pushing with the heels of her hands.

"That's nice," Peggy murmured. Her eyes were closed.

"Thank you."

Laurence finally arrived at the waistband of Peggy's bikini bottoms. She snapped them playfully.

"Hey!" The brunette's eyes opened. "I was almost asleep!"

The girl laughed.

"And now my ass is tense," Peggy added as a muttered aside.

Laurence gently pressed the heels of her hands into Peggy's rump. The older woman inhaled softly.

"This makes it better, maybe?"

Peggy did not respond.

"Is it okay?"

"Sure." Peggy tried to break the tension, joking: "I always charged double for this at the spa."

This time it was the girl who did not reply. She moved the heels of her hands in little circles, watching Peggy's round firm butt jiggle in response.

At length, she slid her hands down to the older woman's legs.

"Your body is very nice," Laurence said in a soft even tone.

"Thank you," Peggy replied, trying to keep a quaver out of her voice.

"You get many compliments?" The girl squeezed Peggy's upper thighs, sliding her hands down and up again.

"Compliments? No, not really. I guess."

"That's a pity." Laurence casually slid her thumbs deeper and deeper into the space where Peggy's thighs touched. "In France, people always tell you when your body looks fantastic. Men, and women too."

Peggy did not respond. She began breathing harder. Laurence gently pulled at the legs to spread them a bit. Peggy did.

At that moment, YuLing ran into the patio area, waving a phone.

The women both jumped. Laurence removed her hands and sat up. Peggy raised her shoulders, remembered her top was off, and awkwardly lowered herself again.

"Phone call," YuLing said. She smiled as if she saw this scene ever day. Turning, the housekeeper departed.

"Hello?" Peggy said into the phone. She set her chin on the chair. "What?"

After a while, the brunette walked over to Laurence, who had returned to her seat at the table. Peggy had reattached her bikini top.

"Sorry about that," Peggy said.

"No problem. Is everything okay?"

"Yeah. That was a lawyer I've hired in Canada. He wanted to know if I'd be up tonight. Seems there's a tax thing to take care of, and the deadline's eight AM tomorrow. He can work late on it but he'll have to fax it to me and I'll need to fax it back with signature pronto. Et cetera."

"He will send it to the fax machine in the office?"

"Yeah."

"Does it have toner?"

Peggy blinked. "I don't know. I didn't think of that."

"I will check." Laurence stood and walked into the house, in her panties.

She returned after a short time. "There is toner, and I checked the paper also. The phone line is connected. It seems to be fine."

"Great." Peggy was sitting in her usual chair. She downed the last of her second drink. "Look at this!" Grinning, she twisted her hourglass hips at the girl. Peggy had used imagination, a rubber band and two paper clips to attach her phone to the side of her bikini bottom.

"That is comfortable?" Laurence sat.

"Comfortable enough."

"It is a good invention." The girl frowned. "Do you know the time?"

Twisting her body, Peggy glanced at her phone's screen. "About six-forty. Why?"

"I wanted to swim." She turned her head and stared at the ocean.

"You're going back to the hostel?"

"Yes, of course."

"Well, you have little time. Do you need to be gone by seven?"

Laurence nodded.

"As long as you're not too long, it'll be fine."

The blonde looked back at Peggy. "I feel like, I must swim hard. I have all this…" Laurence made a frustrated face and flicked her fingers, mimicking someone having a fit. "…Inside of me."

"Oh."

"I do not know if there is enough time."

Peggy said nothing. After a couple of minutes, the girl jumped up. She smiled. "Will you come?"

Much later, at the water's edge, Peggy stared out anxiously. She shielded her eyes from the setting sun. The girl was nowhere to be seen. Peggy tried shouting Laurence's name, but the surf was too loud.

After an endless wait, she saw a silhouetted

form slowly rise out of the ocean. Laurence. The girl pulled her wet hair from her face and shouted something as she approached.

"What?" Peggy yelled back.

Laurence came closer and closer. Finally, when she was only feet from Peggy, the girl said: "I'm sorry I was so long!"

Peggy studied her. The French girl eyes were bright. She huffed and puffed, having pushed herself through what had clearly been a workout. Her smile illuminated her face as if a light shone behind it; this was the only time when the girl appeared completely happy. Peggy smiled. "I'm glad you had a good time."

Laurence laughed. She threw her head back and began twisting seawater out of her long blonde hair.

Peggy glanced down. The white panties had turned translucent with the soak. The girl's blonde bush showed through.

When the older woman finally raised her eyes, she saw Laurence smiling at her. "Yes?" the girl said in a teasing way.

"Uh. Yeah. You know, it's nearly eight. You'd better hurry—can you still make the bus?

The girl shrugged. "Probably not."

"I can drive you."

"If you wish. I don't want to impose."

"No, you're not. But if you want to go back…"

"It does not matter. I only do not wish to be a

burden."

"You're no burden!"

Laurence laughed again, still giddy with her swim. "Then, maybe I stay one more night. But I go back tomorrow, definitely, and stop... what do you say, 'mooch?'"

"'Mooching.' And you're not. C'mon, let's get you inside." They turned and walked to the house. Peggy touched her phone's screen. "I'm ordering two pizzas for dinner. One white pizza with mushrooms and one pepperoni. I was waiting to hit the order button until you got back. If you got back. Does that work for you?"

"Thank you, yes," the girl said. She skipped over sand in the dim light. "I swam to the raft."

"Oh really?"

"Yes." Laurence sighed dreamily. "The raft is not so far."

"I dunno. You were out there a while."

"I did not stop. I swam further than the raft. Much further."

Peggy stared. "Just how far out did you go?"

"I do not know. I almost..."

"What?"

Laurence said no more. They ascended the steps to the patio.

Upstairs, they faced each other in the hall— Peggy in her bikini, Laurence in her panties. The girl held her jeans and shirt in one hand.

"Here we are again," Peggy said.

"Yes." The girl smiled. She brushed damp hair

over her ear.

"Getting to be a habit," the older woman said after an awkward pause.

"Shall I put my clothes in the washing machine?"

Peggy looked at her guest's face. Laurence had a wicked smirk. "That's okay," Peggy replied. "I'll do it."

Keeping her eyes on her employer's eyes, the girl pushed her wet panties down her hips. They slid down onto the carpet. She stepped out of them, picked them up, and dangled them over the bundle of clothes in her hand, still looking into Peggy's eyes.

"C'mon," the brunette said after a long pause. She laughed.

Laurence dropped the panties and rolled her clothes into a tight bundle. Naked, she affected a solemn, military stance. She handed the bundle to Peggy, who accepted it.

"May I hug you?" the girl asked.

After another pause, Peggy answered: "Sure."

Laurence stepped forward and embraced, as she had the night before. This time however, she pulled her arms tighter, squashing her naked body into Peggy's. Setting her face on Peggy's shoulder, she began to rub her employer's back, gently. "Not very good massage, no?" the girl said.

Peggy did not reply. With her free hand she reciprocated, sliding her palm up and down Laurence's bare back.

They remained that way for minutes. Not a word was spoken. One of the girl's hands snaked up under Peggy's hair. Her fingers slid into the base of the thick black locks, rubbing. The older woman's eyes fluttered shut. Laurence pulled her chin in, her warm mouth pushing against the crook of Peggy's neck.

The doorbell rang, startling them both. The French girl jumped back.

Peggy made a face. "Pizza."

"Ah." Laurence nodded, then smiled. "Perhaps I should get it?" She twisted her naked form into an arms-spread-wide "hello" pose.

"Good idea. I think the guy would say it's on the house."

The girl laughed.

"I'll get it," Peggy said.

When she entered the kitchen carrying pizza boxes she found Laurence wearing the robe the girl had been in that morning.

"Hey," the host said. "Want to eat in the living room? We can watch some TV."

"Fantastic."

"Bring some plates and napkins, and whatever you want to drink."

Later, after they had eaten their fill and watched an episode of *Talk Soup* (Laurence: "So funny!") and *The Real Housewives of Beverly Hills* ("These are real women?"), Peggy turned off the television. She and Laurence sat on the big couch, enjoying the easy silence. Without looking,

64

Peggy's hand slid across the cushions toward Laurence; the girl reached and touched it. They held hands, each moving her fingers slowly over the other's.

"I can relate to some of those Real Housewives, you know?" Peggy said finally.

Laurence turned to her, puzzled. "How?"

"They just seem…" Peggy hesitated. "Trapped. I guess that's the right word. They have all this stuff…"

"Trapped?"

"Yeah. Like a gilded cage. You know?"

The girl studied her closely. "You are serious?"

"Yeah."

"Peggy… do you have children?"

The woman looked down. "No."

"You have a job?"

"No."

"And no husband?"

"I think you know the answer to that one. To all of them, actually."

Laurence had become very intense. "Peggy, you are free. How can you say you are like a trapped person?"

"What's the matter with you?"

"Because I do not understand. You're more free than… anyone."

Peggy looked down again. After a moment, she replied: "I just never… I don't know. When I was younger, your age, I had ideas about being a great masseuse. And that didn't work out. Then I tried acting—did I ever tell you that?"

Laurence shook her head.

"That's why I changed my name. And that didn't work out. And then I got married, and that didn't work out, either. I don't know, I just…"

The French girl waited.

"I feel like… At one time, I was ready to take over the world and be reckless and crazy and nothing would stop me. Now, I'm a single woman living in a big house and… I feel the exact opposite of reckless and crazy. I feel like anything can stop me."

Peggy seemed to have withdrawn into herself. Laurence slid closer to her. She squeezed her hand. "You are the same you. This person who was wild and confident, she loved life, yes?"

Peggy nodded.

"Life is still out there," Laurence said. She gestured to the window. "All you must do is go. It will find you, and you will feel this again."

"Easy for you to say." Peggy smiled and squeezed back. "You're so young and beautiful. You have everything to live for."

This statement seemed to throw Laurence for a moment. Then she recovered, and smiled. "You are beautiful, also."

Peggy looked down again. When she finally turned back to Laurence, the girl was staring at her body. Peggy still wore her bikini.

"Always, I wanted this." The girl nodded at Peggy's figure.

"Huh?"

"I have no…" The girl sighed. She withdrew her hand from Peggy's and made a cupping-breasts gesture. "I am not curvy."

"Are you crazy? I always wanted to look like you. Slim and athletic—there are way, way more girls who want to look like you than like me."

Laurence smiled. "But you are attractive."

"You're attractive, too."

The blonde slid closer. "But you are sexy."

Peggy stared at the girl's lips. "You're sexy, too."

Laurence moved no closer. She waited. After a moment, Peggy turned her body, the sofa cushions squeaking as her bare legs slid over the leather. Her face approached Laurence's.

And then Peggy's phone rang.

They stared at each other, frozen, their noses an inch apart.

"The lawyer, with the fax?" Laurence finally asked.

"Naturally." Peggy made a sound of exasperation, leaning back and grabbing her phone from its makeshift holster on her hip. "Hello!"

Almost an hour later, Peggy pressed the "Send" button on the office's fax machine. It buzzed and began eating pages of documents that sat in its feeder.

"Finally," Peggy said.

At her side, Laurence grinned. "Taxes are

important."

"No kidding. The government has the power to take everything away from you, if you make a mistake."

The girl chuckled. "And then, we are out on the street."

Peggy laughed with her. "If anybody's gonna repossess my stuff, I'd rather it be Philippe."

Laurence's laughter died on her lips. A strange hard light blazed in her eyes.

"Oh, shit," Peggy said. "Hey. I'm sorry. I'm really…"

"Good night." The French girl turned and walked to her room. Peggy heard the door close.

\* \* \*

Early the next morning, when Laurence stepped into the hall, she found her freshly laundered clothes folded neatly on the floor in front of her.

The two women worked almost in silence the entire day, only speaking to each other when necessary. At five o'clock sharp, Peggy looked at Laurence directly for the first time. "Are you coming to the pool?"

The girl glanced up from her documents, slightly startled. "Yes. Do you want me to leave?"

"Of course not. I just didn't know if you wanted to leave."

Laurence shook her head.

"Okay, then."

On this afternoon, Laurence kept her clothes on. Sitting in their chairs with their drinks, she and Peggy made strained conversation. Finally, they stopped talking. The silence filled the air.

"I wish to apologize for last night," the French girl said finally. She stared at her drink.

"No, I'm the one who's sorry," Peggy said in a rush. "I can't believe I brought him up like that. My dad, he always said that I couldn't see my foot without wanting to shove it into my mouth."

The girl shook her head, a slow, mournful pan back and forth. "I was so rude. After everything you have done for me, it is... unforgivable."

"Don't say that."

"It is the truth."

"I think you're being a little hard on yourself. You've suffered a really major shock. Personally, I'm amazed you've done as well as you have." Peggy looked down at her own drink. "Which makes me feel even more guilty."

Laurence looked up, her eyebrows knitted in puzzlement. "Guilty?"

"You are in this very vulnerable place, and... I should not have taken advantage."

The girl set her drink down on the table. "Taken advantage?"

"Yes."

"This is a bit condescending, no?"

"What?"

Laurence closed her eyes. She breathed in, then out. "I cannot say this any other way. I

69

wanted to kiss you. I have wanted to kiss you before all this... thing. Before my father died."

Peggy stared. "Since we're baring our souls, let me ask: are you gay?"

The girl shook her head.

"Okay. Me neither. Do you like... do you like to fool around with girls?"

Unexpectedly, Laurence laughed. She laughed long and hard, releasing tension. Finally: "I do not know. I have never tried it. And you?"

"Same here." Peggy paused. She looked at the girl. "So what are we doing?"

The blonde shrugged. "I like you. And I think maybe you like me."

"Well, yeah. But..."

"You have heard of the sexuality continuum?"

"What's that?"

"It says that men and women do not have their sexuality as a binary thing, gay or straight, either this or that. It is on a spectrum. Many different possibilities. And people, their place on the spectrum can move."

"Doesn't that make sexuality... sort of uncertain? Like, a person could jump into bed with anybody, at any time? I don't buy that."

"No, I don't either. But still." Laurence gave Peggy a shrewd grin. "And I have always thought that women are more flexible than men."

After a long pause, Peggy said: "I can't believe we're talking about this. After last night. I didn't get much sleep, by the way." A thought occurred to her. "Did you?"

"Yes, I slept well."

"It must be great to be French."

Laurence shrugged again. "I do not see so much of a problem with us."

"But if we… and especially if you are about to be…"

"What?"

"Nothing."

"Married?"

Peggy did not speak.

Laurence sighed. "Yes."

"Don't you think that is sort of a problem?"

"He and I agreed before. Well, no, he said, and I agreed."

"Agreed about what?"

"Until the day we are married, we may do whatever we like with whoever we like."

Peggy stared. "O-kay."

"His decision. And I know, I know," she said with sudden vehemence, "he is FUCKING so many girls. Probably right now, this minute. He's doing it while he can, before the wedding, while I am gone."

"Seems to me he couldn't find a girl hotter than you."

Laurence smiled. She looked away.

"Seriously."

"When I protested this decision, he told me, 'You are the one who is leaving. If you want to marry me today, marry me today.'"

The older woman frowned. "I don't understand…"

"He wanted to be married immediately. From almost the first date. He is older, you see. He wants children. He has none. He said I am selfish for wanting to wait."

"When did you meet him?"

She considered. "Four months ago."

"And that's too long to wait?"

The girl closed her eyes, shook her head and made an exasperated sound. "I decided I would take three months and travel to California. I had wanted always to go. Movies, beaches. I had this idea. You know? And after we are married, probably I will have no chance, with children and that life. He fought me so hard. He told me I only wanted to come to California so I could fuck surfers."

Peggy stared.

"So finally," Laurence continued, "he said, 'You may do what you like, and I will do what I like.'"

"And… have you fucked many surfers?"

Laurence looked at her.

"Kidding. Jeez," Peggy said.

"When I received the email about my father dying, I called him first. Do you know what he said?"

Peggy waited.

"He said, 'What do you want me to do about it?'"

The older woman massaged her temples.

"Then I called you," Laurence concluded.

"Can I ask you an honest question? And I mean this seriously. Honestly."

"Of course."

"Why are you marrying this guy?"

The girl looked down. "He is strong. And he is successful. He is not sensitive, it is true, but he has had a hard life and has made much out of nothing." She sighed. "And I love him. Not crazy, I-miss-you-all-the-time love, but something I have never felt for another man."

Peggy said nothing.

At length, Laurence added: "I am ready to talk about the funeral now."

"Just get it all"—Peggy made a vomiting motion—"out at the same time, huh?"

"Yes." Laurence turned to the table. She gulped down both her margaritas in succession. When finished, she asked: "Can we walk on the beach?"

"Sure, if you can stand up," Peggy joked.

They strolled along the water's edge. As usual, they had the beach to themselves. Laurence spoke of the funeral. Only a few people had attended— her stepmother, a few of her father's business acquaintances, her aunt, and herself.

"There was complete indifference," Laurence said. "In that room. With the casket there. And it was cheap, his wife had chosen the cheapest thing. I was the only one who cried. The only one!"

"I'm so sorry," Peggy said. She offered her hand. Laurence gripped it tightly.

"And I thought..." Laurence paused, closed her eyes, and took deep breaths as they walked.

Peggy looked ahead, making sure the girl would not stumble. "Take your time."

"I thought that if it was me, in that casket, no one would have cried at all. Not my father, no one."

"Aw, no. That's..."

"Not true? It is true. My father never gave me any kindness. For so long I wondered what I had done. Then I realized he was like that with everybody. And my mother cares only for her social circle. She sent me to boarding school when I was in kindergarten. Kindergarten! When I was small she and my father divorced, she did not even bother to tell me. When I found out, I telephoned him. He said, 'Your mother is a bitch.' He said that to his little child!"

"God, honey..."

"I have no brothers or sisters," Laurence continued, staring forward as the words poured out of her faster and faster. "I was away at schools so long that I do not really know anyone in my family. And they do not know me. I called my aunt in Toulouse, my father's sister, to give me a ride to the funeral. She had not planned to go. She despised him. Then at the funeral my stepmother spoke to me once. She said only that my father's will gave everything to her. I tried to ask her some things, and she turned away. I had nowhere to stay after the funeral and my aunt said there was no room at her house. So I went to a hotel. Do you understand now why I wanted to come back?"

"And... Philippe?"

A bitter tone crept into the girl's voice. "I called him the moment I arrived, before I went through passport control. He said he was busy with business but maybe if I stayed a week, he could see me. Like maybe he could fit it on his schedule."

"I'm sorry," Peggy repeated for lack of anything else to say. They had reached the far breakwater. Still holding hands, Peggy gently turned Laurence around. They began walking back in the direction they had started.

The girl continued, heedless: "And I was thinking, all the time, 'I wish I had not come. I wish Peggy had not wasted her money.'"

"I'm sorry, too. Not for the money, I don't care about that, but I feel terrible that I arranged it. For you to get hurt."

"You could not have known." Laurence looked out at the sea. "I did not know. No, that is not true. I did know. But I did not wish to accept the reality. The coldness, the indifference."

They walked the rest of the way back in silence, hand in hand.

Finally they stopped by the water in front of

Peggy's house. Laurence stared at the horizon. The sun was failing. A pink hue had filled the sky.

Peggy studied Laurence carefully. "Is there anything I can do?"

"You have done so much," she whispered.

"I don't see how."

"Here, with you, I laugh. Nowhere else."

"Wow."

"Yes."

A long pause.

"Anything else? That I can do, I mean."

After a moment, Laurence gave her a long sideways smirk.

Peggy rolled her eyes. "Come on," she said, tugging. They walked back up across the beach to the patio.

By the pool, Laurence pulled off her shirt and removed her jeans. She smiled at Peggy. "This always makes me happy."

"This and swimming." Peggy folded a towel.

Wearing only her panties, Laurence flipped her body with a graceful movement to land stomach-down on a flat lounge chair. Peggy set her towel down, knelt upon it, and touched the girl's shoulders.

Laurence turned her head toward Peggy and clasped the nearer of Peggy's hands. She rubbed Peggy's knuckles gently, staring at the fingers.

"You'll only get half a rub," Peggy joked.

Laurence appeared not to have heard.

Peggy's free hand slowly worked its way down

the girl's back. Laurence sighed, a sound of pleasure. She kissed Peggy's captive hand.

The brunette's other hand kneaded the girl's hips, one by one.

"Touch me there," Laurence said softly.

"Where?"

Laurence parted her legs, still staring at Peggy's fingers.

The older woman hesitated. Slowly, she slid her free hand up and over the contour of Laurence's round butt. After a pause, the palm continued its journey, ever so lightly, down between her legs.

"Inside," Laurence whispered.

Peggy's finger touched the border of the white panties, running up and down along the hem. The girl giggled and bucked. "Tickles. Go inside."

Peggy slipped her hand inside Laurence's underwear, cupping her butt. The blonde sighed. Her eyes closed. Peggy kneaded the firm cheeks for a long time.

"Touch me there," Laurence repeated.

Peggy tried to control her breathing. The masseuse's fingers slid in a slow journey under Laurence's panties down the fissure between her legs, until they touched moist hair. The girl moved her hips up slightly, encouraging her. Peggy slid her hand lower still, then began rubbing the girl's warm vagina.

Laurence started kissing Peggy's other hand, giving each finger a long touch of her lips.

Peggy massaged the girl's Mons Venus. Time passed. The sky grew dark.

Finally, she said: "I have to sit up."

Laurence nodded and exhaled. Peggy had been slightly bent over, with little support from her arms, for a long time. She raised her hands and put them on her hips, wincing as she lifted her shoulders.

Laurence turned onto her side, watching.

After Peggy had performed a series of yoga stretches, she smiled. "Hi."

"Hi." The girl smiled back. Her eyes were warm.

"How are you?"

"I am wonderful. But I must say… rather, I must tell you something."

The words made Peggy visibly anxious. "Okay."

"It is very difficult for me to achieve orgasm," Laurence said simply.

"Oh."

"It has always been so. I do not want you to feel…" The girl's voice trailed off.

"Like I'm not doing something right?"

"Yes, exactly."

"Okay. I wasn't exactly trying, just now. Incidentally."

"Good."

"I was just enjoying the moment."

"Good," Laurence repeated.

"Doesn't it feel weird to you, for us to be

talking about this?"

"No."

"The French." Peggy sighed, wincing again as she turned her torso.

Laurence sat up, setting her bare feet on the tiles. "You are stiff?"

"Yeah, I kind of held that position for way too long. My fault."

The girl rose to her feet. "You should move. Come. Stand. Let me help."

Laurence helped her to her feet. With her arm around Peggy's shoulders, she led the brunette around a circuit of the pool before guiding her down the steps to the beach once again.

Peggy flexed her spine. "I'm fine now."

Laurence removed her arm, sliding it down Peggy's back. Her fingertips touched the bikini bottoms, tracing the border where the fabric cupped Peggy's cheek.

They walked slowly toward the dark water. "I was attracted to you the first day," Peggy said.

Laurence studied her, pleased. "Really?"

"Yeah. At first I thought it was just a girl crush, or something. Perfectly understandable. You are beautiful—"

"Stop." Laurence looked away, smiling. Her hand shifted from tracing the line on Peggy's butt cheek to cupping and rubbing, gently.

"That's just obvious." Peggy placed her own hand on the blonde's rump, running her fingernails with a light touch up and down thin white cotton fabric. "And it was just kind of fun. But then when I thought you were sort of reciprocating, you know, going topless and all that, it kind of short-circuited my brain. I didn't know what to do."

"I became attracted to you also. I felt your interest. I liked it." The women moved closer to each other, hips touching as they looked out at the night sea.

"This is the strangest story," Peggy said finally. She slipped her hand into Laurence's panties, rubbing the girl's ass. "I don't think anyone would buy it."

The blonde laughed and pushed her own hand into Peggy's swimwear. It was a much tighter fit, since the custom-made bikini bottoms fit Peggy's curves perfectly. Laurence grimaced. "This does not work," she said.

"Sorry." They looked at each other and smiled, a long lingering glance. Then a particularly loud wave caught the blonde's attention. She pulled away.

Stepping forward a few paces, the girl dipped her toes into a rush of eddying water. She turned back to Peggy, excited.

"Swim with me. Swim with me!"

Peggy bit her lip. She looked at the ocean. It roared from the blackness beyond the first few feet of surf she could discern. Glancing up, she said: "There's not even any moonlight."

"We will be fine. The currents are not strong. I

have swum many times. Yes?" Even in the dark, Peggy could see the French girl's eyes shining. A kind of feral happiness had taken hold, the night sea's effect on her. Laurence's eagerness and impatience seemed to fill the deserted beach.

"We will go only as far as the raft," she continued, seizing Peggy's hand. "The raft is maybe five minutes. No more. Peggy! This moment, take it. With me. Life"—she gestured at the blackness in front of them—"is there. Not here."

"I can't. Laurence... I... I can't." Peggy seemed ready to cry. She looked down, afraid.

"Peggy, share this with me." The French girl touched her face.

The older woman looked up. Laurence kissed her once, then again. They stared at each other. Then they embraced, kissing for the first time.

Finally, Laurence pulled away. "This is the moment," she whispered. She pushed her panties to the sand, and stood naked.

Peggy stared. After a long pause, the brunette reached behind her back and unclipped her bikini top. She slid the straps off her arms and let it fall. Locking eyes with Laurence, she slipped her swimsuit's bottom down and off.

Laurence smiled. She held out her hand. Peggy took it. They turned and began walking into the dark water.

It suddenly was knee-deep. A large wave loomed before them, advancing like a moving wall.

"Dive!" Laurence cried. Peggy followed her lead, diving headfirst with her into the yawning curl. The sea churned them. Peggy lost her grip on the girl's hand. She rose to the surface; her toes could still touch the bottom. She looked around wildly. "Laurence!"

"Over here." Peggy saw a dim form ahead, waving to her. "Quickly. We must go past these waves. After a few meters, no more waves. Come!"

Peggy hesitated. The ocean moved her body, pulling her back to the shore. Another swell ahead lifted Laurence up and then down. It kept advancing toward Peggy, rising higher. Peggy took a deep breath and extended her arms. She dived into it, kicking hard.

After a few seconds of desperate swimming, she actually collided with Laurence.

Peggy righted her body, treading. She spit water. "Sorry," she gasped.

The French girl laughed. She kissed Peggy with great joy. "Let's go!"

They swam side-by-side, holding hands. After more high swells, the water became calm. "You see?" Laurence asked.

Peggy looked back over her shoulder. She saw the lights of the houses on the beach. The roar and grumbling of waves grew fainter as they swam farther out.

Pitch black surrounded them. Nothing could

be seen ahead—neither sky nor horizon. Peggy gripped Laurence's hand harder.

"*Aie*," the girl said.

"Sorry." She lessened the pressure.

"Are you frightened?"

"Who, me? Swimming in the ocean at night? Where everything looks like one big pot of ink? No way."

"Two more minutes and we are there."

"Okay."

"I remember where it is. Trust me."

"I already trust you. If I didn't, I wouldn't be here."

Laurence said nothing more. They kept swimming, paddling with their feet. A piece of seaweed slid by Peggy, brushing her shoulder. She shivered and kicked harder.

At once a big low object appeared in front of them, stopping their progress. It made lazy slapping sounds as the ocean moved under it.

"Here we are," Laurence said. She sounded giddy. "I will get on, and then help you up. All right?"

Peggy said nothing.

"Are you okay?" The girl asked, worried.

"Yeah. I'm fine. I was nodding. Guess you can't see me. And I can't see you, so that figures."

"Can you hold onto the raft while I get on it?"

With her free hand, Peggy felt around. The area near the bottom of the raft was slimy. She shivered again. Then her hand touched firm decking on top. She gripped it. "Yeah. I'm holding on. Go ahead."

Laurence released Peggy's hand. The girl flipped her body and dove straight down, her feet disappearing under the surface. After many seconds, she shot straight up out of the water like a cork. But she did not time it right; the raft was slightly out of her reach. Laurence crashed back down into the ocean.

"You all right?" Peggy yelled.

"Yes." Laurence spat water, gasped, and pushed hair away from her face.

"Be careful."

"Okay. Again!" A smile was in the girl's voice. She disappeared once more.

On her third try, Laurence managed to land her arms and shoulders onto the top of the raft. She struggled for something to hold onto, her fingernails scrabbling wildly. As a swell passed under them, her edge of the raft dipped down for a split-second; the girl kicked hard and flopped her body like a fish. She managed to wiggle her naked torso up onto the surface. After that, it was only a matter of moments before she lifted her legs too. Spinning gracefully on her hip, she sat up on her knees. "Peggy?"

"Over here."

Soon with Laurence's help, Peggy was aboard. The brunette rolled onto her back, gasped, and closed her eyes.

The deck was made of tough plastic, smooth

and hard. A warm night breeze blew over them; the raft bobbed gently with the ocean's undulations. Occasionally the small clink of a chain tether could be heard.

Peggy finally opened her eyes. She looked back at the shore. The lights of the beach houses were further away but clearly visible. The brunette glanced straight up; the sky was black. A shape near her was sitting up, arms holding knees.

"Laurence?"

"Hi." The girl's voice, in contrast to its earlier euphoria, sounded like a different kind of happiness: peace and contentment.

"Hi."

"What do you think?"

Peggy looked around again, considering. Her head settled back down. "I think this is pretty cool."

Laurence crawled to her, feeling carefully. Lying next to Peggy, she held her hand once more.

They could see each other's faces now. A smile passed between them. Peggy touched the French girl's face, brushing stray wet strands of blonde hair. They kissed.

Their kisses were light, gentle. The ocean moved beneath them. Laurence playfully licked Peggy's lips. "Salty," she murmured.

"Imagine that," Peggy said.

They closed their eyes and continued kissing. Finally, Peggy added: "Correction: I think this is very cool."

Laurence snuggled up next to her, setting her head on the older woman's shoulder. "I have been thinking of this," the girl whispered.

Peggy made no reply. She kissed the blonde head. Laurence slid her palm lightly over Peggy's flat stomach, staring down. After some minutes, she raised her head and shoulders to kiss Peggy again.

They began making out, moving closer. Peggy's mountainous boobs pushed into Laurence's, enveloping the girl's smaller breasts. "It's so sexy," Laurence gasped. She searched for Peggy's mouth in the dark, found it, and kissed her deeply.

Laurence took Peggy's hand and guided it between her legs. Peggy moaned and slid her fingers through the fine pubic hair. The blonde girl kissed Peggy's neck, breathing hard. Her own hand slid down to cup Peggy's big breast. Moving her body so that Peggy could keep rubbing, Laurence licked and sucked the cold nipple into hardness.

"Oh honey," Peggy gasped.

The girl moved her hand farther down, running her fingers over Peggy's navel, before descending into the private area between her legs. Trembling, Peggy parted her knees. The girl's fingers slipped easily over Peggy's smooth shaved mound, running up and down the lips in a slow steady rhythm. Laurence kept sucking; Peggy stopped touching the girl. Her eyes rolled back: "Ohhhh."

The older woman's body began quaking. Laurence, feeling her excitement, slid her fingers faster. "God," Peggy cried. Her body seized, then jerked in the opposite direction. She screamed.

Startled, Laurence stopped. She studied her lover. Peggy hyperventilated, her wet hair draped over the part of her face where her spasms had thrown it. At length, the older woman opened her eyes.

Laurence smiled. "Good?"

Peggy pulled the girl close, kissing her tenderly. "What do YOU think?"

Laurence laughed.

The older woman continued to breathe hard. She closed her eyes. "I come really easily."

"So. The opposite of me!"

Peggy glanced quickly, but Laurence was smiling. "I'm glad," the girl continued softly. "I am happy for you."

"Not fair though, huh?" Peggy grinned, then exhaled.

"Such is life!"

They made out some more. The raft rolled gently.

"Talk about relaxation," Peggy murmured. Her eyelids closed. "You have massage, I have…"

"This?" Laurence slid her hand between Peggy's legs.

The brunette jumped with new sensitivity.

"Sorry." The girl ran just her fingertips over the slick shaved mound, the lightest of touches. "Better?"

"Yes." Peggy sighed. She seemed like she might indeed go to sleep.

Laurence moved her body to lie at a right angle. She set her head upon Peggy's stomach, resting her ear upon her navel. She stared down as her fingers traveled absently over Peggy's Mons.

At length, Peggy sighed. She moved slightly, opening her legs more. Laurence placed her entire hand over the smooth mound, sliding. Peggy did not protest.

Laurence shifted again, moving her head closer. Her fingers began traveling in circles, drawing closer and closer to the top of Peggy's vulva. The older woman began to breathe heavily once again.

The French girl breathed also, sharing her excitement. She lifted her upper body so that her face was directly over Peggy's vagina. She rubbed faster, pulling the strong toned thighs further apart with her free hand.

A low moan issued from Peggy's throat.

"Yes," Laurence whispered. She stared. It glistened in the dark. The women did not even notice a small stray wave that splashed them.

Peggy began moaning, a deep keening noise. She pushed her hips higher. "Yes," Laurence gasped again. "Yes." She moved her face still lower until her breath warmed the area of her attentions. The girl moved her fingers faster over Peggy's mound in a spiral until she rubbed a quick gyrating motion over her clitoris.

Peggy cried out; she reached and grabbed for Laurence, sinking her fingers into the girl's body. Her hips jerked and her vagina almost touched the girl's mouth. As she collapsed she seized the girl's hand, stopping the action. Shivering, she pulled Laurence back up to her.

"No more," Peggy said in a voice so faint it almost could not be heard. "I have to swim back."

Laurence giggled. "It is so much fun."

The woman's eyes opened. "I'm glad you're having such a good time," she said. She sighed and hugged the girl close.

"I am glad YOU'RE having such a good time."

After almost an hour of cuddling and kissing, it was time to go. They stood.

"Whoa," Peggy said as a large swell passed under them. She bent her knees and extended her arms for balance.

"Do not fall," Laurence warned.

"After what you did to me, it's a wonder I don't pass out," Peggy joked. Her big breasts wobbled with the raft's motion.

"Ready?" The girl extended her hand.

Peggy grasped it. "Ready."

They looked at the lights of the beach houses

in front of them. "One... Two... Three!" Laurence chanted. With a whoop, they jumped off the raft together.

Back at the house, after a naked dinner of leftover pizza, they ascended the stairs.

"I must return to the hostel tomorrow," Laurence said as she walked up the stairs naked. "I cannot keep wearing the same clothes every day." Her shirt, jeans and panties were once again spinning in Peggy's washing machine.

"Sure, if you want. Or you could just bring your stuff here," the older woman said.

"Here?"

"Just an idea."

They reached the second floor and walked down the hall. Laurence stopped. Peggy noticed and turned around.

"You are asking me... inviting, to move in?"

"Well, yeah. I mean, if you want to. It's up to you."

"You know I will be returning to France."

Peggy nodded.

"And this does not bother you?"

"I..." Peggy's eyes dropped. She gazed at the girl's nude form, then looked into her eyes again. "This is a big conversation. Do you really want to have it in the hall?"

Laurence said nothing.

"You're welcome to stay here."

"I will think about it tomorrow, maybe."

"All right."

The girl offered a sly smile. "In the meantimes, tonight, shall I sleep… here?" She indicated the guest bedroom.

"'Meantime.'" Peggy shrugged, feigning indifference. "Whatever you want. My bed is little bigger."

"But of course you will be in it."

"I usually am."

"So you are asking me to sleep with you?"

Peggy rolled her eyes.

Laurence giggled. "Okay, I sleep with you."

Trying to suppress a smile, Peggy turned and walked to her bedroom. Laurence followed.

As Peggy brushed her teeth, she glanced at Laurence through her open bathroom door. The girl was studying art on the wall, moving sideways. Then she pushed aside the curtain of a large picture window. The dark night made the ocean outside invisible.

She smiled and turned to Peggy, pointing: "The raft is out there, somewhere."

The older woman smiled back. She rinsed.

Laurence entered the bathroom, but stopped short. "Wow."

Peggy followed her gaze. "Oh. Yeah." A freestanding spacious shower stood in the center off the master bathroom. It was shaped like a cylinder, completely round with a curved glass door. Jets dotted the walls and ceiling.

"I have never seen one like this."

"Came with the house." Peggy yawned. "I

don't know about you, but I've had a long day."
She smiled and approached Laurence, kissing her.

The girl looked again at the shower. "This
seems big enough for two people."

Peggy raised her eyebrows.

In short order, the women were standing
inside it, the ocean's salt on their skin rinsed off
by jets that sprayed hot water at them from every
direction.

"This is fabulous!" Laurence cried.

Peggy smiled and twisted her body to peer at a
console of rubber buttons. "Oh, yeah? Check this
out." She pressed one. The jets all began pulsing
in a staccato massage function.

*"Formidable!"* The girl laughed happily. She
turned her face up to the deluge from the ceiling's
shower, rubbing her face and brushing her hair
back with her fingers.

Peggy kept smiling. "I like to make you
happy."

Laurence regarded her shrewdly. "I also like to
make you happy."

The girl kissed her, snaking her arms around.
Peggy responded. They made out for many
minutes, rubbing each other in a pretext of
rinsing. Laurence took a bar of soap from a wall
cavity and began sliding it over Peggy's round,
firm butt. After a moment, she slid the soap up
and down between her host's legs.

Peggy's eyes narrowed. "What are you doing?"

Laurence was all wide-eyed innocence:

"Nothing." She kissed the brunette on her cheek, then nibbled her earlobe.

Peggy sighed. Her eyelids closed. She moved backward gradually until propped against the wall. Laurence moved with her, replacing the soap into its holder but still rubbing her lover's vulva.

After a short time, the older woman began trembling. "Laurence... you can't just... do this whenever you want..."

Peggy opened her eyes. Laurence's wet face was inches from hers, staring rapt; the girl breathed heavily. Her lips widened with her mounting excitement.

Peggy suddenly gasped and cried out. The orgasm shook her body hard. Finally the tremor that had begun deep inside of her subsided. She inhaled and exhaled, moving the girl's hand away and wrapping her in a bear hug. Laurence kissed her neck tenderly.

In bed, the French girl bounced her bare butt on the California-King-sized mattress. "It is indeed big!"

Peggy sighed. She was exhausted. She walked naked to the wall and turned off the light before crawling under the covers.

Laurence snuggled up to her. "A good day. Yes?" She kissed Peggy on her cheek.

No response. The girl drew her head back, puzzled.

The brunette was asleep. The bedcovers over her followed her curves, rising and falling with her breaths.

The blonde smiled. She slid her arms carefully around her host, then closed her eyes.

In the morning, Laurence awoke to a familiar *thump-thump-thump* noise. Bleary-eyed, she rose out of bed and staggered to the hall.

In the exercise room, Peggy beamed. "Hi!" The older woman was running on her treadmill.

Laurence groaned. The naked girl leaned against the doorway and massaged her temples. "Do you do this every morning?"

"You said it didn't bother you."

"I was being polite."

"Just shut the bedroom door."

The French girl glared. "I'm awake now."

"Good. It's Saturday, and YuLing is off, so you can make breakfast. I'll be done in twenty minutes."

Laurence departed. Peggy heard the bedroom door slam. "I think she's going to sleep in, after all," she added to no one in particular. She grinned and upped her treadmill's speed.

Later, around noon, the two women sat at a sunny table by the bay window. Peggy still wore her sweats; Laurence had changed into her freshly- (and often-) laundered clothes. The girl studied a file folder of Canadian estate documents. Peggy surfed the web on her iPad. The detritus of brunch lay scattered on the table: toast, jam, and butter.

Peggy glanced at the girl. "It's Saturday, you

know."

Laurence did not look up. She made a note on a paper. "Yes. So?"

"Well, you're off the clock."

Puzzled, the blonde looked at her. "What does this mean, 'off the clock?'"

"It means it's no longer working hours. Why don't you take a break?"

The girl shrugged. She returned her attention to the file. "Work is time, time is money, and time not spent working is money lost."

Peggy cocked her head. "Your father said that."

"No, Philippe," Laurence said absently.

"No," Peggy replied in a careful tone. "I'm sure you said it was your father."

The girl looked up again. She stared blankly, then frowned. Her shrug this time was impatient. "My father could have said it. What does it matter?"

Peggy made a face to indicate that it did not matter at all. Laurence returned her attention to the papers.

After a few minutes had passed, Peggy began speaking in a casual voice. "Have I ever told you about my ex-husband?"

"No," Laurence mumbled.

"He was very successful. Roger was so sharp…"

"Then why aren't you still married to him?" Laurence interrupted, eyes on her documents.

"Hey."

The girl made an exasperated sound. She set down her pen, folded her arms, and stared.

"What's the matter with you?" the older woman asked.

"I am trying to work. You only have a few days before you leave and meet your brothers and sisters for the negotiations in Canada. It may seem like most of the work is done, but always there are more things to do, things to check. And I am working 'off the clock' as you say, because I care. About you."

"I appreciate that."

"So?"

"It's just that I was telling a story, and you were being disrespectful."

Laurence tried very hard not to roll her eyes. "Please continue with your story."

"Roger," Peggy continued after a pause, "had all this great stuff going on. I thought any girl in her right mind would be crazy to pass him up. And yet all my friends were telling me I was out of my mind. They were telling me that *I* was the crazy one."

The girl made a polite face.

"And after it was all over... the divorce, the messiness of it, all the trauma, I asked myself, 'How could I have made this mistake?' It took a while, and some therapy, but finally I got the answer."

"Yes?"

"Yes. You see, Roger was exactly like my father. And I loved my father, more than anyone on earth, but, my God, he and I had a very dysfunctional relationship. He was just... incredibly hard for anybody to get along with. I told you how he couldn't keep a secretary for more than a week?"

Laurence nodded.

"By the time he died he'd had more wives than I have fingers. To me he was the most loving, caring, loyal person in my life—but the truth is that the he was also an arrogant, controlling, sometimes deceitful person who had a streak of self-destructiveness. He chose wonderful women, just like the way he chose wonderful investments. He had great taste. But there was no way his marriages could have worked. Or mine, with Roger." The older woman's face flushed. She struggled to control her emotions.

The girl studied her curiously. "So, you blame yourself? I don't understand..."

"No, not at all. I did, once. But now I see what was going on, and I understand it. I had wanted to marry Roger not DESPITE that he was exactly like my dad. I had wanted to marry him BECAUSE he was exactly like my dad. Not in a sick kind of incest way... The dynamic was that unconsciously, or subconsciously, however the brain works, deep down I wanted to resolve all the problems I had had with my father. And so I chose Roger, so I could live it all over again—and maybe resolve it the second time around. But, A., once I understood what had happened, I knew that that was crazy. And B., there could have been no happy ending with me and Roger—no more than my father could have had a happy ending with any of his wives."

Laurence turned her head slowly while still keeping her eyes on Peggy. "What are you saying?" she asked in a be-careful tone.

"Your father. His coldness and indifference— that was, at bottom, his soul, wasn't it?"

"Yes."

"And he was financially very successful also. Right?"

Laurence said nothing. Her body sat very tense.

"Look," Peggy said in a rush. "Look at the similarities. Philippe's all these things. And he's an older man, even. You can't deny—"

"How DARE you," Laurence said venomously. She trembled. "You want me for yourself, and you try to poison—"

"No!"

Laurence sprang up. "How can you say this? You know Philippe and my father are the two subjects in the world that most upset me. Especially Philippe, with this, this thing, here, now, between us. This." She gestured back and forth.

"Aw, no. Laurence," Peggy said, her voice breaking. "You mean more to me than you know—I would never try to poison your mind just so I could—"

Laurence turned and stormed off toward the front door.

"Laurence!" Peggy sprang after her. "Don't you remember saying, on the beach, that you knew but you didn't want to accept—"

The girl flung open the door and whirled around, her face mottled with rage. "And did YOU not hear ME when I said I love Philippe? I love him. I love him! So what if he is cold, he is the part of me I can never, WILL never let go. You take your expert psychology to work on yourself maybe, before you put it on me."

Then she was gone.

\* \* \*

Two days later, Peggy walked into the deserted lobby of a small mission-style building in Malibu. Her shoes clicked loudly on the ancient hardwood floor.

She approached the front desk, glancing at a sign that read "St. Lorenzo Youth Hostel" and, under it, "Reservations Only—No Walk-Ins."

"Hello?" Peggy called out. She tapped a desk bell.

After a moment, a young unshaven man opened the back office door. "Yeah, uh-huh," he mumbled into his cell phone. He shuffled to the counter.

"Excuse me—" Peggy began.

The young man held up a finger. Peggy stopped talking. "Right," he said into his phone. "Dude, hold up a sec. Wait." The clerk looked at Peggy. "Reservation?"

"No, I'm looking for someone," Peggy said. "She's staying here. A French girl. Laurence Duclos. It's very important."

The man pushed his phone into his chest. "I can't let you in. Rules."

"Can you please go and see if she's here?"

"I can't leave the desk unattended."

"Is there someone else who can help?"

"Sorry. No."

Peggy exhaled. "Can you tell me if she's even still here?"

"Sorry, again. By law I can't give out that information."

"She... used to work for me. Do you have an email address for her? I've tried the temp agency she worked with, but they don't have a record of it. I can't believe I never asked her for her email—"

"I don't know. But, again, I can't give out information."

Peggy withdrew a small envelope. "I've tried calling, but you don't give phone messages, right?"

"Right. And the guest phone doesn't accept incoming calls." He nodded to a behemoth lobby telephone with a credit card processing terminal.

"Can I leave this note? I've printed her name

on the front."

"Sure." The man accepted Peggy's envelope.

A long pause followed.

"Anything else?" he said finally.

"No. Thank you very much."

He nodded. Peggy turned away. She heard the man say "Yeah, dude. So anyway, I was thinking…" Looking back over her shoulder, she saw him shuffle back into the office and close the door. Her letter was nowhere to be seen.

\* \* \*

Peggy was placing folded clothes into her suitcase when her phone rang. She looked at its screen and answered. "Hello?"

"Hello."

"Hi."

Long pause.

"You are leaving for the airport soon?" Laurence asked.

"Yeah. I'm actually packing now. Left it till the last minute. Procrastinator Peggy, that's me." The brunette tried to laugh, sounding even more awkward.

"I am sorry I left in the manner I did," Laurence said. She sounded like someone who had rehearsed her lines.

"That's okay. I'm sorry too… I guess I'm just sorry for everything."

"Everything?"

"Well, yeah. Like I said in my letter."

"What letter?"

Peggy made a sound of frustration. "I knew that guy would screw it up. The front desk guy, at your hostel. I gave him a letter for you."

"When?"

"Three days ago, I think."

"No, I never received it."

"Then... why are you calling?"

Silence.

"No, don't get me wrong," Peggy added hurriedly. "I'm glad you called. Super glad. I just, I'm surprised, that's all. Very happily surprised."

"What did you say in this letter?"

"A lot of things. Hey. How are you? Where are you?"

"I am at the hostel." The girl's voice sounded as flat and detached as the first day they had met. "I am fine."

"Oh. Good."

"I'm sorry I left," Laurence repeated. "It was unprofessional."

"What?"

"You have a very important conference with your brothers and sisters. Regarding the estate. Our agreement was not only that I would help you organize the documents, I would remain behind and help you over the phone when you were there."

Peggy nodded. She began walking around her room.

"If you still want my help, I am happy to

help," the girl said in a neutral tone.

"You mean... you'll come back?"

"Yes."

"You know the plan was that you would live here while I was away. I don't know when I'm going to need to talk to you—could be day or night."

"Yes, I remember."

"So you'll stay here? At least until I get back?"

"Yes."

Peggy jumped up and down in her bare feet but tried to keep her voice casual. "Okay. Great. Uh, I would come pick you up, but I don't have time—"

"I can arrive in less than an hour. I will bring my things. Will you still be there?"

"Yeah!" Peggy squeezed her eyes shut and silently stomped her foot. "I mean, yes. I'll be here."

When Peggy answered the door, she did a double take. "Wow. You've had some sun."

Laurence entered, pulling her wheeled suitcase. Her skin had turned brown. "Yes. I have been at the beach a lot."

"You should be careful, you'll get skin cancer. Forget I said that. Hi! It's so good to see you." Peggy made as if to hug her, then changed her mind.

"Hello." Laurence's face was expressionless. She shut the door behind her.

"Okay, so, I told YuLing to make whatever

you want to eat of course, and you can go ahead and open my mail while I'm gone. I'll be away for four days."

"Yes, I remember."

"Any questions?"

"Your phone number in Canada, what will it be?"

"Don't have one yet. I'll buy a Canadian cell phone as soon as I land. I'll call the house phone here as soon as I've got it."

"Have you changed any of the files or other information since I left?"

"Nope. I haven't done one thing with them, actually."

"All right. I have no other questions."

"Thank you so much, Laurence. I... I'm really glad you're here."

The girl said nothing.

"And," Peggy continued. She took a deep breath. "I will never, ever say anything about your father or... your fiancé again."

Laurence looked at the floor.

"So! I'm going." Peggy smiled and walked to the garage door. She looked back.

Laurence lifted her hand in farewell.

Over the next few days, Peggy made many calls to Malibu.

"What businesses are there in Saskatchewan?" she asked one evening.

Laurence rose from her office chair and walked to the wall, peering at the push-pin map.

"Only two. Greydon Mining and Pulp Paper Limited."

"Great. Are they public?"

"Of course."

"What's the market cap on those?"

After Laurence had provided all the relevant information, Peggy laughed. "My half-sister Lisa seems to think she only wants to own stuff close to home."

"She lives in Saskatchewan?"

"Yep."

"This is... a remote area, yes?" Laurence glanced at the map.

"So I've heard. You should see her, and her husband. They live in a geodesic dome. For real."

"Aaaaah. So maybe they will be willing to trade a few things?"

"You got it."

"And you will visit them in Saskatchewan of course."

"Hell no!"

On her last night in Canada, Peggy sighed happily over the phone. "Want to hear a story?"

"Yes!" Laurence had over the days grown more animated with Peggy. They had returned to their former intimacy, laughing and teasing each other.

"My youngest sibling. His name is Barry. So automatically, you don't like him, right?"

"Should I not?"

"Absolutely."

"I despise him."

"Excellent. So. The last birthday party my father had, he was in a wheelchair. Couldn't breathe very well. Just a mess, you know?"

"Okay…"

"My half-brother Barry—I don't know why I keep saying half- this or that, they're all my freaking half-sisters and half-brothers. But you knew that already, right?"

"This story is becoming boring."

"Well, listen to this. It's my father's birthday party. Barry shows up. And he's drunk. And all night long, over the merriment and whatever, he keeps badgering my father about his will in front of everybody. At one point, he actually said he needed more money than the rest of us, because he had 'greater ambitions!' And all the guy does is drink and smoke dope. And contract venereal diseases."

Laurence made a face. *"Degolas."*

"Yeah. My father really loathed him. He didn't even think Barry was legitimately his—dad talked to me at one point about maybe making him take a blood test. He suspected Barry's mother cheated on him. The guy looks nothing like my dad—Barry wears a size fifteen shoe and my dad was a little old Jewish accountant, okay?"

Laurence laughed. "So."

"So. Today, I took Barry to the cleaners. Traded a bunch of stuff with him. I made sure my lawyer was standing by and we got everything signed off on."

"You got his Alberta Oil Sands!"

"Honey, please. I got that, and more. Oh, he still has millions, but knowing him he'll burn through it all soon. So it would have been wasted anyway, right?"

"Indeed yes."

"I know it sounds terrible, but I'm so happy." Peggy sighed, a sound of pure contentment. "My father would have been proud of me. I know exactly what he would've said: 'Honey, you're a chip off the old block.' That was his highest praise."

Laurence smiled. "I think it is wonderful. Good for you. I am happy for you and your father, wherever he is now."

"Thank you." Peggy's voice caught.

After a pause, Laurence asked: "So you are returning here tomorrow?"

"Yeah. And, hey."

"What?"

"Don't leave before I get there, okay?"

"I will not leave."

"There's some things I want to talk about… and I wanted to ask—"

"Yes, I will share your bed," Laurence said simply.

"Oh."

"No?"

"No. I mean, yes! That's… great. Better than I hoped. Way better. It wasn't what I was going to ask, that's all."

"What then was your question?"

A long pause. "I don't remember."

"Ah."

"Anyway."

"Anyway."

"I'm really looking forward to seeing you tomorrow," Peggy said softly.

Laurence smiled. "I too look forward."

"Okay, then. I guess that's all."

"*A demain.*"

"Bye."

"Bye."

The next evening, at bedtime, Peggy and Laurence undressed. They chatted casually, trying to ignore the moment's tension.

"So your trip was the roaring success?"

"'A roaring success.' Yes. I couldn't have done it without you." Peggy reached behind her back and unclipped her bra. Her big breasts wobbled as the brassiere fell.

Laurence paused as she slipped off her jeans, staring. Peggy noticed.

The women considered at each other. Laurence stood in her underwear, Peggy in only her panties.

After a long moment, Peggy said: "I've been thinking."

"Yes?"

"I… I missed you. No wait, let me finish. I wanted that closeness with you—sleeping together. That's all I thought about when I was in the bed in the hotel in Ottawa."

Laurence waited.

"But I don't think it's right that we keep having sex," the older woman continued.

The blonde looked at the floor. She nodded.

"I mean," Peggy said, "regardless of whatever... he is doing, two wrongs don't make a right. Right?"

"Right."

"I want the closeness with you. But the sex..."

"I agree. It has bothered me also. I try to be..." Laurence made a blasé motion, fluttering her wrist. "But always I feel the guilt. So I'm glad you say, we stop."

"Good." Peggy exhaled. "So. No nude sleeping."

"I have sweatpants, and a T-shirt."

"I have pajamas."

They smiled at each other, showing mutual relief. After they brushed their teeth, Peggy turned off the light. She slipped under the covers. The women cuddled.

"Good night," Laurence whispered.

"Good night," Peggy said. She kissed the girl on her forehead.

\* \* \*

"MotherFUCKerrrrr...
MotherFUCKerrrrrr..." Peggy moaned in the dark room.

The older woman was straddling the girl's face, clinging to the headboard for balance. Laurence, her eyes closed, ate Peggy with slow sexy movements of her mouth that reflected her deep hunger for her lover. It had been less than ten minutes since lights-out and their agreement about not having sex. Later they would argue about who had touched who first, who had been inappropriate first, who had seduced whom. But right now they were completely focused on each other.

"Oh God, honey," Peggy said in a high-pitched voice. Her eyelids snapped shut and her head jerked back. She bucked hard but Laurence held on.

"Honnneeeeeeee…" Peggy emitted a sudden gasp, then a scream. Finally, she managed to extricate herself from the blonde girl, collapsing onto the mattress.

When she finally had stopped shivering, she opened her eyes. Laurence was sucking her big breasts, insatiably.

"I thought we agreed we wouldn't do this," Peggy whispered.

The girl did not reply. She began rubbing her fingers between Peggy's legs as she sucked her nipples into pebbles. The older woman made a despairing sound. She managed to pull her lover up. They made out hungrily, feeling each other's heat.

\* \* \*

At the sunny dining table, the two women ate breakfast in silence. They did not look at each other.

"I am going to the supermarket, madam," YuLing said, beaming. If YuLing felt any surprise concerning Laurence's new status of sharing the home, and evidently the bed, of her employer, the housekeeper kept it to herself.

"All right," Peggy called after her. The garage door opened and closed.

After a long pause, Peggy looked out the window. "Well, the forecast said it might rain."

"Yes," Laurence said. She glanced out another window evasively. "It looks like the rain may come."

"Clouds are dark."

"Yes."

Another excruciating pause.

"So," Laurence finally said. "Are there more things to do with the estate?"

"Oh. Yes!" Peggy rose to her feet, grateful for the distraction. "A bunch of things. We have to sort out all the contract paperwork from the meetings. Ownership papers... Lots of stuff."

"So you need me to stay here a bit longer?" Laurence asked, poker-faced.

"Yes," Peggy deadpanned. "Unless you need to leave?"

"No, it is fine."

"When do you return to France?"

"The twenty-second."

"Two weeks."

"Yes."

"Okay. Well, I'm sure we can get everything squared away by then," Peggy said.

"Very good."

"So I'll meet you in the office."

"Okay."

After a work day of sorting papers and inputting numbers, an afternoon of drinks by the pool and (for Laurence) a swim in the ocean, and YuLing's dinner of pork chops (which she left in a warm oven since she went home every day at six)… Peggy and Laurence undressed in Peggy's bedroom, making small talk once again.

"Okay," Peggy said suddenly. "We have to not touch each other tonight. For real." She paused as she was about to unclip her bra. "Stop staring!"

Laurence turned away quickly.

Peggy slid the bra off her shoulders and arms, and donned her PJs. "Like I was saying," she said. "I feel really bad about last night."

"Me too," the blonde said.

"So this time, we sleep on opposite sides of the bed."

"Okay."

"It's a big bed. We'll have plenty of room."

"Yes. I agree. I just agreed, before," Laurence muttered. She slid her jeans off, turning away from Peggy and bending over.

Peggy stared at Laurence's panties pulled tight over her cute heart-shaped rump. The panty lines did not line up with her bikini bottom's tan lines. Two clear strips of demarcation between white and nut-brown skin ran diagonally up the girl's cheeks like a V.

Peggy's mind wandered. "So…"

Laurence looked over her shoulder, puzzled. "So, what?"

"Um. So! We have to leave each other alone."

The girl shrugged. "I am tired, anyway. Last night… no rest. I will be asleep before you turn the light out I think."

\* \* \*

Peggy turned Laurence's naked body over, face-up. Even in the darkened room, a light sheen of perspiration could be seen on the girl's tanned skin.

"Oh my," Peggy whispered. "Whatever has happened to you?"

Laurence would not, or could not, reply. As Peggy adjusted her guest's limbs, the girl offered no resistance. She lay like a rag doll.

After lights-out, Laurence had kept tossing and turning. Peggy had asked what was wrong. The French girl had complained that Peggy had offered her no massage that day, and that as a result her muscles could not relax. After a short argument over whether Peggy had been right not to offer, the older woman had agreed to give the girl a quick back rub.

The massage had begun with Laurence's

clothes on. And one by one, the articles had been removed, each time with a comment by one of the women about how the massage would be better as a result. Peggy had luxuriated in touching the girl's naked body, sliding her hands up and down her, until Laurence had become as limp as a noodle. Finally, Peggy had slid her hand down between the girl's parted legs and gently massaged her vagina, just like on the day by the pool. Laurence had sighed, over and over. While rubbing, Peggy had kissed and licked the skin of the girl's shoulders and neck. That was when sweat broke out over Laurence's body.

And now she lay face-up, unresisting, almost unconscious, as Peggy settled between the girl's tanned thighs. The older woman smiled. "I see now what you meant," she said softly. "This is fun." Laurence made no reply.

Lying on her stomach, Peggy shifted her own body slightly forward. The golden fur between Laurence's legs seemed to glitter in the dark. Peggy opened her mouth and slid a finger over her tongue, her eyes never leaving the blonde triangle. Then, with infinite slowness, she traced the finger through the hair, allowing the curls to wrap around and tug at her fingertip. Still Laurence lay as if dead. The girl was completely relaxed.

Peggy rested her cheek against a tanned thigh, allowing her nose and mouth to press into the blonde pubic hair. She inhaled deeply, and smiled.

After a moment, she kissed.

Minutes passed, the women lying motionless in the dark. Peggy stirred, and kissed again. And again. Shifting her body, she ran her lips tenderly over Laurence's labia. The girl moved so slightly she almost did not move at all.

Tenderly, Peggy began to kiss and lick, moving her entire head in slow up-and-down bobs. Eventually she whispered: "Who knew you tasted so good?"

Laurence groaned. She spread her legs wider.

Peggy licked the girl deeper and deeper, taking her time, sliding her hands over Laurence's body, massaging, teasing her nipples into hardness. Peggy was completely in the moment, experiencing Laurence. She did not hurry. It was a beautiful, tender thing they were sharing; Peggy felt aware of being in a precious moment, a moment that would mean something to both of them.

After what might have been hours, or only minutes, Laurence moaned a deeper timbre than before. Her hand snaked over her body to interlock fingers with her lover. "Peggy," she whispered.

Peggy opened her mouth wider, covering the precious area between Laurence's thighs. Eyes closed, she slid her tongue inside and found the girl's clitoris, hard and angry. Peggy sucked the tiny organ, moving her mouth, luxuriating in the feel of her lips sliding over Laurence's wet pubic hair. Peggy moaned. The vibration in her throat carried up her mouth and into Laurence; the girl touched Peggy's head with her free hand.

Laurence's breathing grew faster and deeper. *"Je t'aime,"* she whispered so softly Peggy could not hear. *"Je t'aime."*

Peggy's hand slid up and down the girl's tanned body, unconsciously massaging, touching, guiding Laurence ever-closer to orgasm. Peggy was a conductor, playing the girl's body like an instrument.

Laurence began to tremble; Peggy ate her harder, with mounting excitement. After a beat, Laurence's back arched; she screamed a low loud long sound.

When her tremors had subsided, Laurence looked down: Peggy's face was still between her legs, licking her insatiably.

"Peggy," Laurence gasped. "Please. Hey!" She pulled at Peggy's with a frantic movement.

As if waking from a dream, the older woman looked up.

"Come to me," the girl breathed.

Peggy crawled on her hands and knees to lie next to Laurence. The blonde held her tightly.

"You're shivering," Peggy said. She kissed her forehead.

For many minutes, Laurence did not reply. Then: "Thank you."

Peggy giggled. "You're welcome." She kissed the girl's sweaty face.

"Do not laugh." Laurence opened her eyes; they looked bluer than ever before. "I have never felt that. Never like that." She snuggled her head into Peggy's arms. "Never like that," she whispered again.

Peggy held her. They closed their eyes. In moments, they were asleep.

\* \* \*

The following evening, at bedtime, the women stood looking at each other from opposite sides of the bed.

"It is too strong," Laurence finally said.

"Yeah."

"Perhaps I should sleep in the guest room."

"Don't say that."

"I am serious. What can we do?"

"Come here," Peggy said.

The girl approached. Peggy placed Laurence's arms around her neck. "You have four days left. Right?"

The blonde looked down and nodded.

"Why don't we just make the most of them."

Laurence looked up again. "We let go?"

"Yeah."

The girl's smile lit up the room. "Yes, then. If you are happy."

"I am."

They began to kiss.

\* \* \*

Peggy woke up in the dark. Feeling around, she let her eyes adjust to the gloom. She was alone in the bed.

Sitting up, she scanned. Laurence was nowhere to be seen.

With a short hop she bounced to the bed's side, then off onto her feet. She pulled on a robe. "Laurence?" she called. Her eyebrows knitted. She called again, anxious.

After exploring the upper floor, she descended the stairs before stopping short.

Laurence was weeping softly on the sofa, naked. A letter lay on the coffee table in front of her.

"Hey," Peggy said.

The girl jumped. She looked up, wiping tears. "I'm sorry. Did I wake you?"

"No!" The older woman hurried down and embraced her, sitting by her side. Glancing at the coffee table, Peggy said: "That's my letter. The one I left for you at the hostel."

"Yes." Laurence sniffed and wiped her face again.

"What…"

"I read it every night." The girl exhaled. "I leave the bed while you are sleeping and I come down and I read it. I leave it in the cushions, here"—she indicated where they sat—"and put it back when I am done. Then I come up again and go back to sleep with you."

Peggy placed a gentle hand on the girl's

shoulder, rubbing. "I didn't think you received it."

"After I spoke to you on the phone that day, I asked the desk if they had a letter for me. First they said no. I made them check everywhere. I was crazy in a hurry, but I wanted to see. Finally they found it. I took it and ran out with my suitcase… to here."

"The day I went to Canada."

"Yes." Laurence plucked a tissue from a box on the table and blew her nose.

"Well, my next question is… why are you reading it every night?"

"Because it is so beautiful. Peggy!" Laurence held her, sobbing.

"You're gonna make me cry, too," Peggy gasped.

"Do you remember the night I first swam to the raft?"

"Yeah…"

"Did you wonder why I was so long?"

"I thought you got lost, or…"

"No. I swam past the raft, Peggy. Far, far out. Into the darkness. I kept swimming. Philippe, my father's funeral, my family, everything… so terrible. I could not bear it any more. I wanted it to end. I wanted everything over."

"God, honey," Peggy said in a shaky voice.

"But then when I was almost too far to come back, I thought of you. How if I died it would upset you—"

"Upset me? Try, kill me!"

"I know." Laurence touched Peggy's hair, passing her fingers through it. "And I knew I could not do that to you."

Peggy said nothing.

"I came back for you, Peggy."

The held each other a long time.

Finally, Laurence turned her face on Peggy's shoulder to look at the letter. "The things you wrote—about you, about us. I feel the same way. I want to stay," she said in a rush, gripping tighter. "I don't want to leave you. I don't know what will happen, how it can happen, I don't care. I want to stay with you. I love you."

Peggy's lungs suddenly expanded to the bursting point. Seizing Laurence by the shoulders, she looked into her wet eyes. "You do?"

"Yes. Of course."

"I love you too."

They embraced again; the French girl cried, and Peggy simply looked stunned.

*　*　*

Peggy adjusted her bikini and shifted slightly on her chaise lounge. She looked up. No clouds marred the blue afternoon sky.

Laurence exited the house, approaching. As she walked she pulled off her shirt.

Peggy sat up with an abrupt movement. "Well?"

Laurence ignored her. The girl unclipped her

bra and yanked off her jeans to expose a bikini bottom. She would sunbathe topless, as usual.

Peggy banged on her chair, getting the girl's attention. "WELL?"

Laurence made a sour face. "He said nothing."

"Nothing?"

"I explained it—how we met, everything. I was careful to include it all. I thought, Philippe deserves a good explanation. Right?"

"Right." Peggy nodded a little too vigorously.

"But he did not say a word." Laurence sighed.

"Wow."

"Except at the end."

"Oh?"

"*Bonne chance.*" The girl regarded her. "That means..."

"Good luck. Yeah, I know that much."

Laurence seemed sad.

"What's wrong?"

"It was... no emotion. The coldness. Awful." She sighed again.

"But... aren't you happy you're not marrying him?"

"I wish I never had—"

Peggy waited.

"I feel stupid, only," Laurence said finally. "That's all."

Peggy smiled. "Hey. I know what'll cheer you up."

The girl gave her a sidelong look.

The older woman rolled her eyes. "Not

THAT. A swim."

Laurence grinned. "But it is not evening, yet."

"Sometimes it's better to swim in the light."

The girl thought about it. After a long pause, she nodded.

Peggy rose. Laurence followed. They smiled at each other. Clasping hands, they walked down the patio stairs and over the beach, toward the ocean, together.

The End

Thanks for reading! If you have time, please review *Night Swimming*. I read every review, and I appreciate honest feedback!

If you enjoyed this book, you may also enjoy

*The Beard*

By Anne Eton

When tall, pretty Kelly interviews at Washington D.C.'s premier LGBT-centric lobbying firm, she claims she has a girlfriend. Nothing could be further from the truth; she's never even kissed a girl. Kelly's hired. However, a suspicious co-worker keeps inquiring about her girlfriend. To keep her lies straight, Kelly bases her fictional partner on Anna, an aggressive, gorgeous lesbian friend of a friend. But when the firm's annual Christmas party looms, Kelly's forced to produce her mysterious girlfriend. The real Anna agrees to be Kelly's "beard"—her fake date. But at the party, alcohol flows... and Anna's all over Kelly. Kelly pretends to her office mates that her "girlfriend's" advances are perfectly normal—even as she feels her resistance to the beautiful woman melting away.

*The Beard* is a comedy with sexy scenes and some explicit passages.

Excerpt follows!

*The Beard*

Excerpt:

Kelly stumbled, tipsy. Anna guided her with a sure hand to the office supply room, opening the door and escorting her inside.

"Hey! Office supplies," Kelly said with false cheer. She looked around nervously. "You need some gel pens? Ha, ha!"

Anna smirked. She shut the door behind them and pressed the doorknob's button, locking it.

"Or paper clips, or toner," Kelly babbled, casually backing away. "It's a regular Staples in here!"

"Yes," Anna replied. The blonde gave Anna a sexy look and flipped a wall switch. The room went dark.

"I think we should talk about expectations," Kelly said in the pitch black, as if discussing the price of a car. "I admit, I did sort of use you for my own ends…"

"Yes."

Kelly felt Anna's hands. The tall girl backed away; she came up against waist-high pallets of paper boxes.

"You see," Kelly gasped, "I know we're supposed to be pretending that you're my girlfriend—"

"Yes… yes…" Anna murmured. She began slipping Kelly's dress up as the taller girl moved awkwardly against the immovable cartons.

# Also by Anne Eton

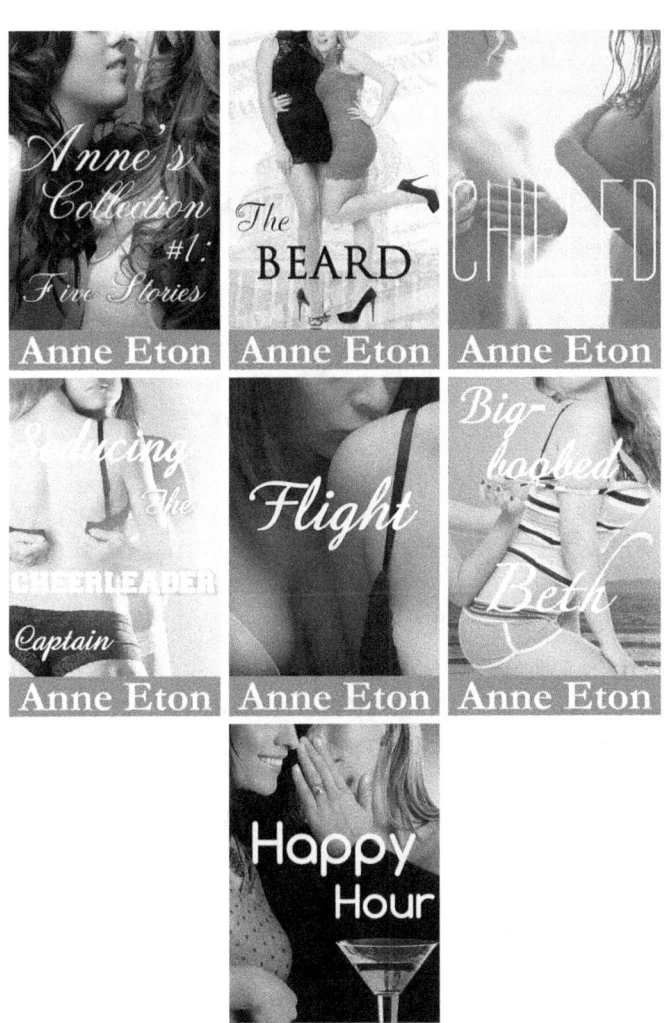

# ABOUT THE AUTHOR

I write first-time F/F erotic romance. I love what I do!

If you would like to know when I publish new books, please join my New Release Mailing List, at my site! I don't share my readers' email with anyone, for any reason.

www.anneeton.com

Thanks for reading!

Anne